BOWIE'S
SILVER

Other books by Kent Conwell:

BOWIE'S SILVER

•

Kent Conwell

AVALON BOOKS
NEW YORK

PRINTED IN THE UNITED STATES OF AMERICA
ON ACID-FREE PAPER
BY HADDON CRAFTSMEN, BLOOMSBURG, PENNSYLVANIA

To the memory of Jim Bowie and his silver,
a fascinating story about which we will
never know the truth.
And to my wife Gayle.

Chapter One

Cam Judson slouched lazily in his saddle outside the Cattleman's Bank of La Grange, one leg hooked around the saddle horn. A Bull Durham cigarette dangled from his lips. He shifted uncomfortably as the hot sun baked his shoulders.

Despite the heat, Cam couldn't resist grinning at his good fortune to latch onto this small band of cowpokes, the leader of which supposedly possessed a waybill to the lost silver of Jim Bowie.

More than once around a campfire at night, he'd heard stories of Bowie's lost cache of Spanish silver, thirty mule loads of it up north around the old San Saba mission. He'd always figured the story was just that, a story and nothing more, until the day Cam saw the waybill.

While he didn't recognize any details on the waybill, he decided to throw in with the small band on the chance the map was genuine.

His grin broadened. Luck, he reckoned, had

finally grabbed hold of his shirttail. The big payday he had always sought was just within his reach. And with that payday would come his dream of a small ranch with a few hundred head of prime stock.

He glanced longingly around the small village of La Grange. Riding in, Cam had noted the land looked fertile, the townsfolk friendly, and the bustling town far enough south that the winters wouldn't be too bitter, not like they were up in the Texas Panhandle where it could get colder than a mother-in-law's kiss at the North Pole.

He nodded contentedly. Yep, after they found the silver, he reckoned he'd come right back here and find himself a ranch and perhaps a fine woman, and not one of those Montgomery Ward Catalogue women either.

Suddenly, his traveling companions burst from the bank. The leader, Latigo, tossed an object at Cam, leaped into his saddle, and shouted, "Every man for his self!"

Cam grabbed reflexively at the bag that slammed into his chest, almost unseating him. "What the—" On either side, horses squealed and pawed the air as their riders whipped them away from the hitching post. He was still stammering when the boom of a shotgun sounded in his ears.

When Cam looked over his shoulder, he saw a man wearing a vest and boiled shirt in the door of the bank, swinging both barrels of a twelve-gauge shotgun in his direction.

Instinctively, he yanked his bay around, slid from the saddle, and squatted in the off stirrup as he sent his deep chested horse racing down the rutted street.

Behind, a hail of lead that hummed like a swarm of bees chased him. At the end of the street, he rounded the corner sharply and came face-to-face with four startled horsemen. Their animals reared and whinnied as he raced through them, heading for the thick oaks and hickories along the Colorado River.

He glanced at the bag in his hand. In faded green letters on the outside of the white canvas bag were the words, *Cattlemans's Bank of LaGrange*. His eyes grew wide in disbelief when he squeezed the bag and felt the crinkle of paper bills. Cursing his luck, he jammed the canvas bag inside his shirt.

Cam leaned low over the neck of his galloping horse. He clenched his teeth in frustration. He didn't want to run, but he had no choice. The infuriated posse would massage his neck with a hemp rope without even giving him the opportunity to explain he had no hand in the robbery.

Upon reaching the broad river, he raced north through the giant hardwoods, hoping to throw the posse off his trail. He had no idea where his three traveling companions were, but they were the last worries on his mind at that moment.

When the good Lord created the Colorado River, He included thousands of hiding places along the river and in the surrounding limestone hills. And the posse seemed to know them all, spooking Cam out of a half-dozen or so.

Late afternoon, he stood motionless beside his pony in a dense thicket of cedar. Gently, he pinched his pony's nostrils as the thundering posse pounded across the flood plain, kicking up billowing clouds of dust. "Easy, boy," he whispered when he felt the nervous horse jitter about. "They missed us again."

After the posse disappeared into the forest beyond the flood plain, he glanced to the setting sun in the west. He had eluded three posses. He was no genius, but he didn't have to be wise as a tree full of owls to know his luck couldn't hold much longer. He had to light a shuck out of the country.

When the last echo from the hoof beats died away, he swung into the saddle and lit out along the posse's back trail, grateful for the long-legged bay on which he was mounted. Three times today, the bay had taken him beyond the reach of the posses. Three times, Cam had dodged a necktie party. Three times the good Lord had smiled on him. The chances of it happening a fourth time were slim to none. And Slim was on the way to Fort Worth.

Staying within the tree line along the river, Cam headed south, away from the posses. He kept an anxious eye on the golden orb of the sun, mentally trying to push it below the horizon, desperately praying for the safety of darkness.

Shadows from the surrounding hills lengthened from across the open flood plain, stretching their fingers toward the ancient hardwoods through which he rode.

He desperately tried to come up with a solution to his predicament. The townsfolk would never believe he was not part of the robbery, that he was completely unaware of his companions's plans.

Nope. If he tried to return the money, they'd take

it with one hand and, with the other, shove him up the hemp stairway to heaven.

Keeping his eyes moving in the growing darkness, he rode warily, the crunching of his pony's hooves in the carpet of fallen leaves and the squeaking of saddle leather the only sounds breaking the brittle silence.

Suddenly, the sharp crack of a rifle shattered the silence, followed instantly by the splat of a slug ripping out a chunk of tree trunk beside his head.

Without hesitation, Cam threw himself forward on the bay's neck and dug his spurs into the startled horse's flanks. Seconds later, the bay was in full stride.

With the pounding of hooves echoing in his ears, Cam glanced over his shoulder. Less than fifty yards behind, half-a-dozen angry cowboys drove their horses after him. Clenching his teeth, he urged his pony faster. He muttered a curse. "Where in the blue blazes did they come from?" Those blasted posses were thicker than horse flies in a cow yard.

Shadows deepened within the profuse stand of trees that were now no more than darker shadows. As surefooted as his bay was, it was only a matter of time before he slammed into a tree or dropped into a gully.

Making a hasty decision, Cam jerked the bay to his left, toward the river. He tightened his legs around the animal's belly, clutched the reins with one hand, and with the other, grabbed the saddle horn. "Get ready, boy," he muttered, driving the straining pony for the bluff overlooking the river.

One instant, they were on solid ground; the next, hurtling through the air to the river fifty feet below.

Cam steeled himself for the impact.

Halfway down, he slid out of the saddle and, seconds later, slammed into the river. Blindly, he clutched at his horse, twisting his fingers into the animal's tail as the game pony swam for the far shore.

The posse reined up on the bluff and peered into the inky blackness below.

"He's down there!"

"Maybe the fall killed him."

One cowpoke turned to the deputy leading the posse. "You think he's dead, Luther?"

With a shrug, the deputy turned his horse to the trail leading down to the river. "Only one way to find out."

Even as they spoke, the moon eased over the horizon, bathing the river with a golden glow.

"Look. Yonder," shouted a posse member. "There he is. Climbing the bluff."

"Shoot the no-account thief," another screamed, levering a cartridge into his Winchester and firing at the nebulous shadow climbing the far shore.

Cam hunkered against the neck of the bay as the struggling animal scaled the steep slope. He clenched his teeth, expecting the jarring impact of a lead plum at any moment. To his surprise, he topped out on the bluff unscathed and vanished into the shadows cast by the great oaks and hickories.

Shafts of moonlight lanced through the canopy of

leaves overhead, providing muted illumination. Cam cut south, then reined up in a tangled thicket and waited.

Within minutes, he heard the pounding of hooves. They drew close, then began to fade until finally all he could hear were the chirping of crickets. To the south, a rabbit squealed as an owl sank its claws into the tiny animal.

After a few more minutes, he descended the bluff, swam the river, and headed north. Once he was certain he had eluded the posse, he could head back to his old stomping ground in Arizona Territory.

The same hot sun that baked Cam's shoulders outside the bank blistered the small group of mourners at San Luis Cemetery on the banks of the San Antonio River not far from Tres Toro Plaza near the heart of San Antonio. The hard ground reflected both the debilitating heat and the withering glare of the unrelenting sun, a sun that sucked moisture from flesh, turned skin to leather, and dried spit before it hit the ground.

Milly Barrett blinked back the tears and hugged her younger brother, Ira, and sister, Ellie, to her as the pallbearers lowered their father's pine casket into the hard-packed ground. Part of her ached for the loss of the one person who had stood between her and the town, but the other part remained alert for the hidden murmurs, the sly whispers, and the furtive undertones that were bound to surface now that he was dead. With the stoicism of her Indian mother, she kept her eyes fixed on the grave.

Slowly, the small group of mourners drifted

away, but Milly and her siblings remained until the last clod of dirt had been scraped off the hard ground and packed into a neat pile on top of their father.

As two Mexican laborers packed the dirt, a third turned to her, removed his sombrero, and bowed. "Soy muy arrepentido, Señorita. Vaya con Dios."

She permitted him a faint smile and brief nod. His expression of sympathy and gentle blessing was the only one she and her brother and sister could probably expect. Keeping her eyes on the grave, she whispered to Ira and Ellie. "Time to go home."

They departed the cemetery and walked down the middle of the dusty road, squinting against the blinding glare of the scorching sun reflecting off the white-washed adobe dwellings lining the street.

"Don't look around," she muttered harshly to the children.

With each step, their feet kicked up balloons of dust, but they kept their eyes forward, ignoring the curious and hateful eyes watching from the darkness of the open windows on either side.

When they rounded the corner to their house, her heart leaped into her throat. She felt Ira and Ellie hesitate, but she tightened her arms about their shoulders and urged them to keep walking.

In front of the entrance to their neat adobe stood the sheriff and their landlord. Grim wrinkles furrowed Sheriff Milo's sun-darkened face in sharp contrast to the smug arrogance curling the landlord's fat lips.

Sheriff Milo nodded and touched his fingers to

the brim of his hat. "Miss Milly. Ira, Ellie. Sorry about your Pa. He was a good man."

She bit at her lip, hoping the pain would stay the tears. "Thank you, Sheriff," she whispered. Her wary eyes met the landlord's. "Mister Dickens."

Dickens looked at the sheriff. "Do your job, Sheriff."

Clearing his throat, Sheriff Milo pulled a folded sheet from his shirt pocket. "Sometimes I don't like some of the things I got to do in this job, Miss Milly. This is one of them." He handed her the paper.

Without opening it, she looked back to the landlord, her green eyes cold with disdain. "You didn't waste any time, did you, Mister Dickens?"

The rotund man blustered. "It's my property. I can do what I want with it."

Milly hugged Ira and Ellie to her. "And you don't want half-breeds living in one of your houses, do you? Strange," she added, a touch of sarcasm in her voice, "you never told Pa that."

The sheriff gave Dickens a look of disgust, then shook his head and grinned weakly at Milly. "You got to the end of the week, Miss Milly. That's all the time I could get for you. Sorry."

She nodded. "Thank you, Sheriff. Pa thought highly of you." She took a step forward. "Now, if you gentlemen will excuse us, we have some packing to do."

Dickens stumbled as he hastened to step aside. Sheriff Milo chuckled.

Chapter Two

Once inside the cool adobe, Ira, 13, frowned up at his older sister. His lips quivered as he fought to hold back tears. "Where are we going, Milly? What are we going to do?"

Ellie, two years younger than Ira, looked on hopefully.

Milly forced a smile. "Go where no one knows us."

Ellie frowned. "Are we really half-breeds, Milly? We don't look any different than others."

Milly shook her head, her blond hair bobbing behind. "I don't understand how it happened, Ellie, but the three of us take after Pa. For some reason, none of Ma's blood shows in us." She paused, then added. "I'm proud of Ma, but people treat half-breeds different. Wherever we go, we must let people think we are white, like them. That's why we can't afford for anyone in San Antonio to know

10

where we're going. People like to gossip, especially hurtful gossip."

"Are we going on the stagecoach?" Ellie asked.

Milly shook her head. "No. Someone on the stage might know us." She paused. "I've been thinking about what we should do. We'll buy a buckboard, head west toward Gonzales, then swing back north to New Braunfels. According to Pa, New Braunfels is a German community. With our blond hair, we'll fit right in." She held a slender finger to her lips and looked at them both. "You mustn't say a word to anyone. You hear?"

Ira frowned. "But, what will we do? How can we live with Pa gone?"

Milly threw her shoulders back. Her eyes grew narrow with determination. "I'll take care of you. Don't worry."

Ira's frown deepened. "But, how?"

"I went to school with the nuns. I can teach. I've read in the New Braunfels newspaper that they have a school called the New Braunfels Academy. I can teach there."

Three days later, Milly and the children clattered into New Braunfels from the south, the same time that Joe Brock and his gang rode in from the north.

Charley Lister, a whiskey-ravaged lunger, pulled up beside Brock. "What kinda' town is this?" His bloodshot eyes searched the street for the nearest saloon. "It don't look none like Austin."

Joe Brock's coal black eyes blazed fire at the older man. "You blasted well get drunk tonight, and you'll wake up in the morning with your ears hanging from your saddle."

Lister shrunk back, cringing. "Aw, Brock. I ain't going to get drunk. That last time was just a mistake."

Behind them, Salmon Hatfield and Hez Clutter chuckled. Hatfield said, "You bet, Lister, and we all know Texas ain't never hot in the middle of August."

Brock held up his hand. "This here is a prosperous community. From what I hear, they're hard-working Germans and they be mighty religious and suspicious. We play our cards right, we might set us up a comfortable little place here while taking care of more important business down in San Antonio." He scooted around in the saddle and glared at the three of them. "Anyone who throws a hitch into my plan, I'll put so many holes in him he'll look like a windowpane. Understand?"

The three understood. Brock had pounded his plan into their thick heads time and again. They would establish a residence in New Braunfels, work local jobs, and on the shadowy side, relieve some of the San Antonio gentry of their gold and silver.

Hez Clutter, just barely eighteen and filled with all the energy of a wet-behind-the-ears pup, grinned. "Sure hope they got some German women here who ain't so religious."

Hatfield shook his head. "Women is going to be the death of you, boy. You ain't never going to hit twenty-one."

Clutter laughed. "Maybe not, but I'll sure have me some fun."

Brock glared at him. "Have your fun in San Antonio. Not here. You hear me?"

Clutter tried to outstare Brock but finally dropped his eyes.

Brock's words were brittle. "I said, do you hear me?"

Clutter nodded. "Don't worry, Brock. Anything goes wrong, it ain't going to be me what caused it."

Cam lost track of how many days he had been riding northwest when the echo of a gunshot rolled up from the canyon below. He reined up behind a thick cedar near the rim of a rocky bluff.

Bound for Arizona Territory where his Pa and Ma had died when he was fourteen, he figured he was almost beyond the Texas Hill Country, a rugged area of sheer cliffs, thick growths of cedar and oak and pine growing up through the limestone cobbles, slashed with cold, clear streams of sweet water, and populated by abundant wildlife, the variety of which even the Garden of Eden might envy.

The gunfire continued. Warily, he peered around the cedar, searching the rocky valley below. A sparkling creek, its limestone bed twinkling through the clear water, tumbled down the valley. To the north, he spotted a single cowpoke hunkered behind a sharp upthrust of white limestone. Even as Cam looked on, the cowpoke touched off two rapid shots into the underbrush across the creek. A saddled horse lay on the rocks behind him.

Puffs of smoke appeared from the underbrush and the echoes of the shots reverberated off the rocky walls up and down the canyon.

Hastily, Cam searched the rim on which he stood, but it appeared all the combatants were below. He shook his head. "Know the feeling, partner," he muttered, feeling kinship with the one cowpoke battling off an untold number of foes.

As he looked on, white puffs of smoke from black powder rifles drew closer to the lone cowpoke. Cam counted at least four, maybe five, all spread in a semi-circle that was slowly closing in on the unfortunate cowboy.

For a moment, Cam hesitated, questioning the wisdom of sticking his nose in another's business, but he remembered how he would have gladly taken any help a few days earlier when he was desperately seeing to elude those posses.

"Well, Cam," he muttered as he shucked his Winchester. "You ain't done nothing stupid since the bank robbery. Might as well see what happens."

Shucking his Winchester from its boot, he climbed down and tied the bay to the trunk of the cedar. He knelt behind a tangle of briars near the rim and, without hesitation, squeezed off a shot just to the left of the last puff of smoke, preferring to scare rather than kill whoever was holding the rifle. In quick succession, he touched off three more shots.

Below, the surprised cowpoke jerked around and peered up. Cam waved. The cowboy waved back, then turned back to the job at hand.

The valley sounded like the second siege of Vicksburg for a few moments, and then the opposing fire ceased. Down the valley, fleeting shadows ghosted through the straggly stands of stunted oak and vanished, but not before Cam recognized them as Indians—Comanche, he guessed; that being the predominant tribe in Texas as far as he knew.

Cam led his bay along a narrow trail that twisted to the bottom of the bluff. When he came face-to-face with the cowpoke whose bacon he had pulled from the fire, he froze.

On the cowboy's chest was pinned a badge. A lawman.

Now you gone and done it, Cam, he angrily chided himself.

The older man grinned broadly and stuck out a meaty hand. The tips of his handlebar mustache hung below his lips. "Partner, you ain't got no idea how plumb tickled I am you come along. Them Comanche was figuring on making me deader than a beaver hat. Name's Luke Potter."

The lanky cowpoke hesitated, then took the proffered hand. "Folks call me Cam."

Potter nodded to the north. "I'm sheriff up in Menard about ten or twelve miles thataway." He shook Cam's hand enthusiastically. His gray handlebar mustache bobbed up and down as he nodded. "Yes, sir. Mighty glad you come along."

Cam forced a grin and made an effort to remain calm. He tried to convince himself there was no possible way the sheriff could have heard about the bank robbery so soon. Most of the telegraph offices were in the larger cities. He reckoned Waco was probably the closest, and it had to be over a hundred miles to the east. "Glad I could help, Sheriff," he replied, trying to keep his eyes off the shiny badge on Potter's chest.

"Yes, sir," Potter said, rolling his broad shoulders. "You be an angel from heaven. A blessed angel from heaven."

Cam glanced over his shoulder in the direction the Comanches had disappeared. The hair on the back of his neck bristled. "I don't know about you, Sheriff, but I reckon we best make ourselves scarce. Those Comanche might have kin nearby."

The grin faded from Potter's face. "You're plumb right about that." He glanced around, then shrugged. "Well, Cam, looks like we got to ride double a piece. Joe Preston's ranch is a few miles west. I can get a pony there, and then we'll head on into town." He removed the saddle and gear from the dead horse and stashed it in the underbrush. "I'll come back later for this."

Just before sundown, Sheriff Potter and Cam crossed the San Saba River at a shallow crossing and rode into Menard, a small village of stone and clapboard buildings. Potter reined up in front of the jail. "You got to be mighty tired, Cam. Least I can do is fill your belly and give you a good night's sleep." He nodded across the street. "Miz Garrison runs a clean boarding house and serves up solid grub."

A young deputy hurried from the jail. He looked at Cam curiously, then turned to the sheriff. "Sheriff. I been looking for you."

"Well, you found me."

The younger man glanced at Cam hesitantly, obviously reluctant to speak.

Potter continued. "Ezra, take this gentleman over to the boarding house and tell Miz Garrison to fill his belly and give him a room for the night. The town's good for it."

Ezra frowned. "But, I need to talk to you. It's important."

"Fine. Do what I said, then come on back and tell me whatever's chawing at you."

"But—"

Potter snapped at the young man. "Now!"

The young man made quick work of setting Cam up with a room for the night. As soon as he passed Sheriff Potter's instructions on to Mrs. Garrison, he turned and departed, leaving Cam standing in the middle of the lobby.

The youth's obvious agitation stirred Cam's concern. Had the young man recognized him? His hand drifted to the butt of his Colt.

"This way, Mister—" Mrs. Garrison hesitated, a faint frown wrinkling her forehead.

Mrs. Garrison's gentle words interrupted his thoughts. "Cameron, ma'am," Cam answered, opting to use his first name instead of the last.

"This way, Mister Cameron."

He followed the matronly woman upstairs to his room.

By the time he closed the door behind him, Cam had decided the young deputy could not have recognized him. He wasn't sure just what day it was, but word could not have traveled so far in just four or five days.

He stripped off his shirt and gave himself a quick sponge from the fluted washbowl. "Get rid of some of the trail dust," he muttered to his reflection in the mirror. His stomach growled. He hadn't eaten since early morning. He reckoned he could do justice to one of Mrs. Garrison's meals. Afterward, if matters seemed peaceful about, he'd find a tonsorial parlor for a shave and hot bath.

He paused before heading downstairs to gaze wistfully out the window at the small village and the silent river flowing past. He wondered if he was safe, if, indeed, word had reached Menard. *Relax*, he told himself. The only way his name could be linked to the bank robbery was if one of his traveling companions had been caught, and even then, they only knew him by his last name, Judson.

And he reckoned that while there might not be a heap of Judsons in the big state of Texas, there were probably enough for him to lose himself.

Across the street, the door to the sheriff's office opened, and Sheriff Potter headed toward the boarding house, his broad shoulders hunched forward. Cam's eyes narrowed. He eased his Colt from the worn slick holster and spun the cylinder. It purred like a contented kitten. Dropping the six-gun back in the holster, Cam went downstairs to meet Sheriff Potter.

Chapter Three

To Cam's relief, Potter grinned when they met in the lobby. The sheriff led the way into the dining room, pausing to introduce Cam to the local sawbones, Doc Kelton. "Eat a bite with us, Doc," the sheriff offered.

"Thanks, Sheriff, but my wife filled me up good at supper." He patted his stomach and grinned. "Maybe next time." He pointed to the second floor. "Work to do. Got me a cowpoke up there with a boil on his backside. I could use some help." He grinned.

Potter grimaced. "Say no more, not when I'm sitting down to supper."

Like most western folks, instead of wasting time talking, Cam and Sheriff Potter poured all their energy into putting themselves around steak fresh off the hoof, fried potatoes, thick red-eye gravy, and hot sourdough biscuits, washed down by steaming cups of six-shooter coffee.

The last sinful delicacy was a thick slab of mock apple pie with a latticework crust topped by thick spoonfuls of rich cream.

Cam leaned back and patted his belly. "If Miz Garrison isn't already married, Sheriff, I plan on asking her."

Potter laughed. "Mighty tasty, ain't it? Why, I've done proposed to her every night for the last five years, and every night for the last five years, she's turned me down cold. Maybe you'll have better luck."

They both laughed.

Cam pulled out his Bull Durham and deftly rolled a cigarette. Potter studied the younger man with shrewd, gray eyes. He'd asked his benefactor no questions other than his handle. Nosing into another's business was considered bad manners, but now Potter had a plan on his mind.

"You heading any place in particular, Cam?"

Cam tensed at the question, then forced himself to relax, hoping the sheriff had not caught the momentary flinch. "Nope." Cam shook his head and tossed the bag to Potter. He casually added. "Reckoned on seeing what the country's like out in the New Mexico Territory." He touched a match to his rolled cigarette. "Maybe on out to Arizona Territory."

Potter leaned back and took a deep pull on his cigarette. "Ever been out there?"

"Nope."

"Hear there's a heap of sand out there. Not much water."

Cam shrugged, every sense alert, wondering where the sheriff's questions were heading. Potter appeared casual, relaxed, but Cam couldn't afford to take a chance on questioning by any lawman. He'd run across some lawmen who were slicker than calf slobber when it came to getting information. "I never heard that," he lied, figuring to lay down a few false trails of his own for the sheriff. "Where I come from in East Texas, we got plenty of water and trees. I don't reckon I ever spent more than a few days without seeing water."

Potter studied him a moment. His face grew serious.

Cam forced himself to appear relaxed, but beneath the table, his hand edged toward his Navy Colt. The sheriff looked like the fox ready to gobble up the unsuspecting chicken.

"You in a hurry to get out there? I mean, you heading for a wedding or a pressing job?"

Chuckling, Cam shook his head. "Not me. Just seeing what new country looks like."

Potter leaned forward, his elbows on the table. "Tell you why I'm asking. You strike me as being a square-shooter. My deputy, Ezra—you met him— well, he up and quit on me. That's what he was all fired up about when we rode in. So, now I need a deputy. I'm offering you the job, Cam. Deputy of Menard, Texas. Forty a month and a bed in the jail." He paused and sheepishly added. "Of course, the bunk in the jail is a mite hard. You might have to throw another mattress on it."

A wave of relief washed over Cam. For a moment, he was speechless. Finally, he found his voice. "You don't know me—nothing about me."

The sheriff stubbed out his cigarette in what little gravy remained in his plate. "You could have rode on by today. You didn't. That's the sort of jasper I like having at my side. Well, what do you say?"

Part of Cam cautioned him to ride on out of town; the other, to stay. Of course, one mighty slick advantage of the deputy's job would be that he had a straight pipeline to the law and all its information. If something broke about the bank robbery, he'd be in a good spot to hear of it well in time to light a shuck out of town.

Abruptly, he pushed to his feet and stuck out his hand. "You got yourself a man, Sheriff. One question."

Potter took his hand. "Shoot."

"Do I have to sleep in the jail tonight, or can I have that soft bed upstairs?"

That night, before he dropped off to sleep, Cam figured he had found himself in a situation that might help him wiggle out of the jam he was in.

On top of that, he might even like the idea of deputying. He thought back to the days long ago when his Pa scratched to make a living on the outskirts of Tucson. They were dirt poor, living down in the barrio with the Mexicans, and he could still fill the shame he felt when white folks in Tucson referred to him as that Judson boy that lived down with the Mexicans.

He grew up resenting it, and after his parents died

of cholera, he and his boyhood chum, Patch Mabry, headed for Texas.

The weather in New Braunfels around the first of October was unpredictable. One day called for shirt-sleeves, the next a light jacket.

Milly and Ellie were busy in the kitchen putting together the evening meal. While Milly had been unable to find a teaching job with the New Braunfels Academy, she had picked up several students for tutoring on the recommendation of the headmaster. That income, combined with the little Ira made down at the livery, kept them going.

In the short time they had resided in New Braunfels, they had worked hard, paid their bills, and, to protect their secret, kept to themselves, traits appreciated by the diligent and frugal community. From time to time, neighbors dropped off an extra haunch of venison, or a few hen eggs, perhaps even a chicken.

The three hoarded their meager funds, carefully depositing any unencumbered coin in their slowly growing repository for an emergency.

Ellie set the table, casting curious glances at her older sister. For some reason, there was a glitter of excitement in Milly's eyes, but when Ellie inquired the reason, Milly simply shook her head and said. "You have to wait until your brother is here. But you'll like it."

Minutes later, Ira stormed into the small house, his face red, drawn with fear. A wild look was in his eyes. "Milly. He's here. I saw him. I saw him."

Milly forgot her own excitement. She grabbed Ira

by the shoulders. "Who? What are you talking about?" But deep down, a queasy feeling churned in her stomach. She prayed she was wrong.

Ira sputtered. "He come into the livery. I hid when I saw him." He looked up into her eyes, pleading with her to tell him he was wrong. "He's here."

"Ira!" Milly spoke sharply. "Stop acting like a baby. Who's here?"

"Old man Dickens, our landlord back in San Antonio."

Ellie gasped.

The words tumbled from Ira's lips. "I saw him. Milly, he's here. He's here. He—"

Milly dug her fingers into her brother's shoulders and shook him hard. "Ira! Hush up. Hush up. You hear?" She paused, then in a softer voice. "Now, tell me what happened."

He squeezed his eyes shut and tried to slow his heaving chest. "Okay. I was pitching hay down from the loft when he rode in. I wasn't sure it was him at first, but I hid anyway. It was him. Dickens."

"Go on," Milly urged. "It might be he's just passing through." But she wasn't convinced.

"I laid down up in the loft. I could hear him talking and asking questions."

"About what?"

"He was asking if there was any houses for sale. He said he had thought about buying houses here in town to rent out like he done back in San Antonio."

Ellie looked up at Milly, confusion reflecting from the small girl's eyes. "He won't come here, will he, Milly?"

An icy hand clutched Milly's heart. "He might, sweetheart. We're renting this house from the Hammonds. If he talks to them, he might decide to look at it."

Ira bit his bottom lip. "He can't do that."

With the stoic resolution of the western woman, Milly softly replied. "Yes, he can."

"But, what are we going to do?"

Milly put her hands together as if in prayer and pressed them to her lips. She knew what they could do and still preserve their secret, if they had the time.

"Ira. Did he say he was coming to look now? Or just thinking?"

Puzzled, the young boy stared at her. "What do you mean?"

"I mean, is he looking now, or just thinking about looking?"

He shook his head slowly. "I don't know."

Milly sat at the table and gestured to the chairs. When they sat, she said. "Now, listen. We don't have much choice. If Dickens is looking now, he'll probably find us. But if he's only thinking about it, maybe we'll have time to leave before he finds us."

Ellie spoke up in a thin voice. "Leave? Where?"

Leaning forward, Milly's eyes once again gleamed with excitement. "I had a surprise for you two. Reverend Wesley at the academy got a letter from a small town about two weeks north of here. A place named Limestone. They want a teacher. He wrote them about me, and I found out today, they want to hire me. All we have to do is get up there. We'll have to sell the buckboard and buy a wagon."

The smile faded from her lips. "The problem is that the job doesn't start until December. That means," she added, "we need to stay here another few weeks if we can."

"What if we can't, Milly?"

She forced a faint smile. "Let's face that when we come to it, all right?"

Excitement showed in Ellie's eyes, but Ira's were filled with apprehension. He said. "What if Dickens tells the preacher we're half-breeds? You think he'll still give you the job?"

A cloud of worry filled Milly's eyes. "I don't truly know, Ira. We've been sorely disappointed by people before. The preacher seems to be a good and decent man, but many a good and decent man hates half-breeds. That's why we got to pray Dickens is just thinking, not ready to start doing." She hesitated and studied her younger brother. "And that's why you must slip back up in the loft in the morning. Don't let him see you. Find out what you can."

Next morning, thirty minutes after sunrise, Ira slammed through the kitchen door. "He's riding out. He's going back to San Antonio. He said he'll be back next month."

Milly felt as if a huge weight had been lifted from her shoulders. She smiled at Ellie and Ira. "The Lord smiled on us, youngsters. By the time Mister Dickens comes back, we'll be long gone."

Joe Brock downed his whiskey and slammed the empty glass on the table. "Boys, pickin's are gettin' mighty thin. What with the questions the sheriff's been asking around the last couple weeks, we'd have to have the brains of a grasshopper to keep on hanging around here."

Charley Lister lay snoring on his bunk, his breath reeking of stale whiskey. At the table, Clutter and Hatfield glanced at each other.

Hatfield spoke up. "What you got in mind, Brock?"

Brock studied them a moment. "I heard down at the livery today that a wagon train of supplies is heading out in a few weeks, up through the Hill Country to Fort McKavett. They need some guards. That's us. We'll lay low until then."

He paused, grinning at the confusion on his men's faces. Young Clutter cleared his throat. "What the blazes is at Fort McKavett? All that's out there is Comanche and desert."

"And," Brock added, "thirty mule loads of Spanish silver."

Chapter Four

The afternoon sun sank below the horizon as Cam and Doc Kelton sat on the boardwalk in front of the jail, leaning back in their straight back chairs and lazily smoking Bull Durham.

"Days are growing shorter, Doc," Cam observed.

"Nippier too. Hard to believe we're coming up near the middle of October. Year'll be over before we know it."

"The way of the world, Doc. Just be glad you ain't up in Montana. Hear it's so cold up there, cows give icicles."

Doc Kelton guffawed and rocked forward in his chair. "I got to go back to work, Cam. You take care. By the way, the sheriff's due back from the settlement at Blue Mountain anytime now, huh?"

"I look for him to ride in tomorrow if he hasn't run into no problems."

The Doc studied Cam a moment. "You've done a good job here the last couple months, Cam. I want

28

you to know that the citizens hereabout appreciate it."

The praise surprised Cam. He nodded to the doctor, who was only a few years older than him. "Well, thanks, Doc. Does that mean I'm getting a raise?"

Kelton laughed. "Not hardly." He grew serious. "No, what I'm thinking is that one of these days, the sheriff will retire. He's getting long in the tooth. I can't promise nothing, but I'd say if you're still around, the town could do a lot worse than you."

Cam grinned at the backhanded compliment. "And I reckon I could find a lot worse place to hang my hat."

Both men laughed.

"All we got to do now is find you a good woman," laughed Doc Kelton, rising to his feet.

"Not me, Doc. Women scare me, especially them that are looking to settle down."

Kelton grinned. "Don't tell me you aren't looking to settle down."

Cam grinned. "Not yet."

"You will be," he said. "You will be."

Cam watched Doc disappear down the street. He couldn't help feeling a sense of pride at the compliment, but at the same time, he reminded himself that his time here was only temporary; that if, or when, the bank robbery caught up with him, he'd have to light a shuck out of this country.

He rolled another cigarette. But, until then, he told himself, he was going to enjoy this town and its folks. In the time he'd been here, he had made some friends and taken some steps to rectify his part in the robbery without being so drastic as to turn himself in for a hemp party.

Within a month after taking the job, he had ridden to Mason, thirty miles to the east, on his day off. Sheriff Potter had grinned wickedly when Cam told him he was going to pay court to a young woman he had met just a few days before he had intervened on the sheriff's behalf against the Comanche.

When he rode into Mason, Cam reined up in front of the stage line and posted a small package on the stage to the sheriff at La Grange, a package containing the entire sum of the bank's money in his possession. Inside the package, he expressed his innocence, gave the particulars of his involvement, and made the promise he would continue sending money back until the entire amount was paid off.

Around the first of October, he had ridden into Mason once again, again ostensibly to pay court to the young woman, but instead, he posted half his pay to the sheriff in La Grange.

He hated lying to Sheriff Potter, but he had no choice. He was content with his plan.

Before sunrise, after Doc Kelton had praised Cam's deputying, Cam had ridden north out of Menard to check on some horse rustling on the Edgar ranch. An hour or so later, Sheriff Potter rode in, hungry as a starving lobo.

The sheriff headed straight for Mrs. Garrison's. While he was working on putting himself around a platter of fried eggs, curly bacon, hot gravy, and biscuits, Doc Kelton showed up. "Morning, Sheriff. Saw your pony at the hitching rail."

The sheriff nodded and, around a mouthful of grub, mumbled. "Morning, Doc. Have a seat. How was things around here while I was gone?"

Doc Kelton poured some coffee from the pot on the table. "Quiet. Mighty quiet. Cam did you a good job."

Potter nodded, his mouth full.

Kelton continued. "He's a good man."

Swallowing his grub, Potter grunted. "Yep. Like to keep him around if I can. Maybe he'll marry that gal and settle down."

A frown wrinkled Doc Kelton's forehead. "Gal? What gal?"

Without looking up from his plate, the sheriff replied. "Been courting a little gal over in Mason."

The doctor chuckled. "Why that no-account scoundrel."

"Huh? What's that?" Sheriff Potter looked up sharply.

"Well, he sure led me on," he replied with a broad grin. Seeing the puzzled frown on the sheriff's face, he explained. "Just last night, we was talking. I told him he ought to settle down. He said women scared him. Said he wasn't ready to settle down." He shook his head. "And all the time that rascal had himself a pretty little thing over in Mason. He sure had me going."

Sheriff Potter's eyes narrowed momentarily, and then in a casual voice, replied. "Yep. He can be one to pull your leg, Doc. He sure can."

But not mine, the wise old sheriff said to himself, realizing that Cam had lied either to Doctor Kelton or himself. Luke Potter had toted a badge for over forty years, and he knew a man lied when he had something to hide. *Maybe*, he told himself, *I need to ride over to Mason and find out just what's going on, he told himself.*

That afternoon, the sheriff rode out once again.

Except for the local saloon, the small town of Mason had closed up tight when Sheriff Potter rode in. He pulled up in front of the sheriff's office and went inside.

By the time he sat down for breakfast next morning, he had learned that there was no young woman and that, twice, someone fitting Cam's description had posted letters to the sheriff in La Grange.

The name La Grange rang a bell. Then, he remembered that before he gave his deposition at Blue Mountain, the sheriff from Kerrville had told him of a bank robbery in La Grange. Could there be a connection? Potter grimaced as he stroked his drooping mustache. He sure hoped not.

Before heading back to Menard that Sunday morning, Potter posted his own letter to the sheriff of La Grange.

Chapter Five

Late that Sunday night, Cam sat in the jail reading Jules Vernes's *Twenty Thousand Leagues Under the Sea* in the yellow glow of the coal oil lantern. He had already read the sheriff's copies of *Journey to the Center of the Earth* and *From the Earth to the Moon.*

To Cam's surprise, one of the unexpected pleasures of the deputy's job was Sheriff Potter's library, small though it was. His own Pa had encouraged him to read. Often, when he traveled, he sat in the saddle, reading.

Suddenly the door swung open and Sheriff Potter stomped in, carrying a cloth-covered basket. "Pour us some coffee, Cam. I got fried chicken. I managed to sweet-talk Mrs. Garrison into frying up some special."

Cam lost no time pouring the coffee. "What's the occasion?"

"No occasion. My tapeworm was wrapping

around my spine. I reckoned you might be a mite hungry too."

Reaching for a leg, Cam said. "Heard you rode out while I was up at the Edgar place. We have trouble somewhere?"

"Naw," the sheriff drawled, tearing off a chunk of chicken breast. "Had an errand over in Mason."

"What about Blue Mountain? Everything go all right?"

"Yep. Gave the deposition to the judge just like I knew what I was doing."

Cam sipped his coffee. "Things was quiet here." He paused, then with a grin, added. "Things is usually quiet here."

Potter laughed. "Why do you think I keep this job? Of course, I don't let that on to the citizens. I want them to think they're getting their money's worth."

Both men laughed.

Washing the chicken down with hot coffee, Sheriff Potter continued. "Yep. Trip was worth the time. Them citizens down in the settlement sure gave them rustlers their comeuppance." He shook his head and glanced at Cam from under his eyebrows as he added. "Can't understand them kind. They got to know there ain't no getting away. Like them that robbed that bank down in La Grange."

Cam froze. His heart pounded, but he forced himself to remain casual. He glanced up. "What was that? A bank robbery?"

Sheriff Potter kept his eyes on his plate. "Yep. Sheriff was up from Kerrville. He mentioned it. Didn't know no details."

Drawing a deep breath, Cam reached for his coffee. His hand shook as he picked it up. Quickly, he sat it back down and cut his eyes toward the sheriff, who was intently buttering a biscuit. Cam breathed a sigh of relief. At least, the sheriff hadn't noticed.

The next few weeks were uneventful. There were three or four reports of Comanches running off with horses, a handful of drunken fights at the saloon, but nothing Cam and Sheriff Potter couldn't easily handle.

Around the first of the month, Cam announced that he was riding over to Mason once again.

"You must be getting serious," drawled Sheriff Potter with a crooked grin. "This is the third time you've seen your little gal."

Cam ducked his head. "Naw. Not really."

"What's her name? I might know her Pa."

The question rocked Cam. He had never thought to give her name. "Mary," he replied hastily.

"Mary what?"

Cam thought desperately. "Brown," he blurted out. "Mary Brown."

Feigning a frown, Sheriff Potter stroked his handlebar mustache. "Brown, huh? I know some Browns over there. What's her Pa's first name?" His shrewd gray eyes caught the nervous tics in Cam's eyes, the tics of an honest man, not a hardened criminal.

"I never asked him. I always call him Mr. Brown."

The sheriff grunted. "Well, you take care. See you tomorrow."

Sighing in relief, Cam rode out, reminding himself not to forget her name. He grimaced. Tell one lie, and a jasper had to tell a thousand to back it up. He shook his head at his own lack of imagination. "Mary Brown," he muttered. "It even seems made up to me."

At the stage office, Cam posted his letter. The shipping clerk read the address then looked up. "You from Menard, by any chance?"

Cam stiffened. "Reckon so." He kept his eyes on the clerk but instantly became aware of any movement around them.

"The sheriff wants to see you. Across the street."

Suppressing the alarms going off in his head, Cam remained casual. "The sheriff? Me? Why?"

The clerk shrugged. "No idea. He just told me if someone come in from Menard to send them over."

Slowly, Cam turned, half-expecting a dozen guns aimed at him. Except for a few citizens, the street was empty. "Thanks," he said, leaving the station and leading his bay across the street. With every step, he fought the urge to swing into the saddle and hightail the dickens out of town.

He opened the door and stepped into the sheriff's office, every muscle tense and his hand inches from the butt of his Colt.

A weathered, leather-tough face glowered up at Cam, its keen blue eyes drilling holes in him.

"You the sheriff?"

"Yep."

"I'm from Menard."

A grin burst across his face. "Menard. Good to

see you." He opened a desk drawer. "Got some mail for Sheriff Potter. Sure would be obliged if you'd deliver it to him."

Cam relaxed. "Be happy to, Sheriff. Be more than happy to," he added, feeling as if the weight of the world had been lifted from his shoulders.

The sheriff's name was all that was written on the sealed envelope. Cam slipped it in his saddle-bags and headed home. During the trip, he began to wonder how the shipping clerk had known he was from Menard. Or maybe, he told himself, the old boy simply asked every stranger who came in.

That made sense. Ask every stranger who came in. Cam sighed with relief, then once again cursed himself for getting in such a predicament.

Cam looked on as Sheriff Potter stroked his han-dlebar mustache while he read the letter. When he finished, he studied it a moment longer, then folded it back into the envelope and stuffed it in his hip pocket. "Good news?"

Potter studied the younger man a moment. "Can't say for sure."

Chapter Six

A couple weeks later, while Sheriff Potter and Cam put themselves around a hearty breakfast, the sheriff paused before poking half of a buttered biscuit in his mouth. "Cam, I want you to ride over to Fort McKavett. Supply train with three wagons of settlers coming this way."

Cam sipped his coffee and nodded. "When do I leave?"

Potter speared a couple chunks of fried egg and sausage. "Soon as you can. The sheriff down in Blue Mountain told me they was coming in to Fort McKavett about the end of this month. We need to bring them on over here and then escort them on up to Limestone."

"Whatever you say, Sheriff."

Sheriff Potter grinned at his young deputy. "Good." He paused and grew serious. He lowered his voice. "Now, I got something you keep under your hat. When them wagons come in to Menard, tell the families their wagons need to be greased up good for the trip on over to Limestone."

Cam frowned. "I don't understand. The road isn't all that rough."

Sheriff Potter looked around. "Coby Asplund is the mine superintendent. He's been losing payrolls to hijackers. We plan on putting a secret compartment in one of them wagons and hiding the money inside. Understand now? Understand why you got to keep it under your hat?"

Cam nodded, pleased the sheriff had taken him into his confidence. "Don't worry, Sheriff. Now, how do I find this Fort McKavett?"

"Just follow the river out there. The fort is at its headwaters around a half-day's ride to the west. Now, let's us hush up and do justice to this fine breakfast, and then you can hit the trail. It's a good day for a ride."

The day was perfect for a ride. The cloudless sky was deep blue, the air still and crisp, with just enough of a chill to make a ride invigorating.

Cam rode into Fort McKavett in late afternoon. The stone structures housed the 8th and 9th Cavalry, the well-known Buffalo Soldiers.

He reported to the Officer of the Day in the Headquarters Building and was assigned a bunk, after which a grizzled sergeant pointed out the mess hall. "We's done had our mess, sir, but I reckon Hooby'll find you something solid to gnaw on," said the grinning sergeant as he led Cam and his pony across the quadrangle.

He was as good as his word. Hooby, a massive

black soldier who looked more like he should be bulldogging Mexican steers instead of standing in front of a stove frying up eggs and bacon, put together a tin plate heaped with slabs of venison, curls of bacon, chunks of butter, and wedges of homemade bread. He apologized for the grub being cold. "We's done cleaned up the mess for the night. But come morning, I guarantee you a steaming hot breakfast you ain't never going to forget."

The breakfast was all Hooby promised. Afterwards his eyes half-closed, Cam squatted against the side of the mess hall out of the wind, soaking up the sun, smoking a cigarette, and luxuriating in a full stomach.

Suddenly, his eyes popped open, and he forgot all about the choice breakfast settling in his stomach. He rose to his feet and squinted at the distant rider heading his way across the valley. There was something familiar about the way that cowpoke sat the saddle.

Cam ambled a few steps away from the mess hall and tugged his John B. Stetson over his eyes against the morning sun.

Abruptly, the rider pulled up and stared at Cam. Then, with a whoop and holler, he yanked off his hat, waved it like he was swatting bees, and spurred his horse.

When that first holler rent the still, crisp air, Cam knew who the rider was; Patch Mabry, his boyhood chum and riding partner since they were both old enough to fork a horse. Old Patch.

Cam's initial delight quickly vanished, replaced

with a healthy dose of aggravation. He shook his
head and growled a curse. Blast! Why did Patch
have to show up now? Cam lifted his eyes to the
heavens and muttered. "You just got to make it hard
on a body, don't you, Sir?"

"Cam!" Patch's voice carried about the pounding
of his pony's hooves. "You old son-of-a-gun," he
shouted, reining up and leaping from the saddle.

He grabbed Cam in a bear hug and swung him
around. "Are you a sight for sore eyes! How long's
it been? Five, six years?"

Cam glanced around hastily, seeing just how
much attention was turned on them. To his relief,
no one was paying them mind. He grinned at his
old friend, noting from the patches on his partner's
clothes that Patch was still tight with a penny.
"Something like that. Come on. Tell me what you
been up to," he said, taking Patch's arm and leading
him away from the mess hall.

Patch pulled back. "Hold on. I got to report to
the head honcho at this here fort first. I got me a
supply train coming up, and I need to know where
these blueboys want it."

"Supply train? You got some women and children on it?"

"Yeah. How'd you know?"

"Believe it or not, I'm a deputy over in Menard,
back east. The sheriff sent me to escort the women
and their wagons to town. From what I understand,
all three are going on up to a small mining settlement by the name of Limestone."

Removing his battered hat, Patch beat it against
his leg. Dust billowed from the hat as well as his

worn jeans. "That's what they told me. One of 'em is named Barrett, Milly Barrett. She's going over to teach. The others, Mrs. Keith and Mrs. Morrison, they're going to meet their husbands. Mrs. Keith," he continued, "she's got a right pretty daughter, name of Penelope. Right pretty."

Cam arched an eyebrow. "Uh oh."

Patch ducked his head. "Nothing like that."

"Come on," Cam said, nodding to the headquarters, "I'll show you who you need to see."

Patch grinned. "Sounds fine to me, and then I'll treat you to a long drink of good whiskey. I'm drier than a duck in Arizona."

Cam held him back. Lowering his voice, he said. "I'll explain later, but right now, I'm going by the last name of Cameron, not Judson."

"You what?"

"I told you, I'll explain later. Now, let's get you to the Officer of the Day."

Upon leaving headquarters, Patch pulled Cam around to the side of the white limestone building. "All right. What's going on with you?"

Cam glanced around. "I got trouble," he muttered. "Big trouble." Quickly, he detailed the events of La Grange.

When he finished, Patch shook his head and whistled softly. "I reckon you're right, partner. You got trouble. What are your plans once you pay off the bank?"

"Beats me." Cam shrugged.

With a frown, Patch studied his old friend several

moments, and then an easy grin erased the grimace on his face. "Come on. I'll buy you that drink now."

Upon leaving the saloon, an hour later, Cam and Patch watched as the supply train topped the last rise and headed into camp. He noticed the outriders, grizzled jaspers.

"Joe Brock and friends," Patch offered without enthusiasm. "Hired on in New Braunfels." He shook his head. "They did their job. I can't complain, but they just don't seem the type to ride nursemaid to no wagons."

Cam studied the men as they went about the business of closing down the wagon train. He ambled over to the wagons and introduced himself to the ladies and their children. "Just call me Cam, folks."

Patch nodded to the two boys, Victor Keith and Ira Barrett. "Them little fellers been our wranglers from time to time. Done a good job too."

Cam nodded to them, and the two boys beamed. He looked back to the women. "We pull out bright and early in the morning, folks. That way, we should be in Menard by nightfall."

Milly Barrett stepped forward. "How is the trail to Menard, Mister—I mean, Cam?"

He remembered Sheriff Potter's plan. "Not bad. The trail on to Limestone is rougher, so I been told. We'll grease your axles and hubs up real good in Menard. Probably have to lay over a day or so. Reckon you could use it," he added with a grin.

That night, while Cam and Patch sat by the campfire, smoking and reminiscing, Joe Brock sauntered up.

Patch nodded to Brock. "Cam, this here is Joe

Brock. Him and his boys rode up with us. Joe, this here is Cam—" Patch hesitated, then hastily said. "Ah, Cameron. Cam Cameron. We've knowed each other since we were younkers. Came out of Arizona Territory together when we was fourteen or so."

Brock eyed Cam warily. "Pleased to know you, Deputy. Makes a body rest easier knowing the law is around. Cameron, huh? I knew an old boy named Hank Cameron down in South Texas. Any kin?"

"Afraid not. Never been down thataway."

Brock grunted. "You ever been to San Antonio? You look familiar."

Cam shook his head. "Afraid not."

Patch invited Brock to squat. "Coffee's hot. You and your boys are welcome to toss your soogans around the fire if you've a mind."

Brock poured a cup of coffee. "Right hospitable, Patch. You was a fair wagon-boss on the drive up. Much obliged for the offer, but the boys and me got us a small spot yonder under that mesquite." He glanced at Cam and nodded to Patch. "Good man to work for."

Cam grinned, measuring the big man across the fire from him. "I'll remember that."

Shrugging his thick shoulders, Brock said. "Hear you're taking them women on east tomorrow. I'd appreciate if you'd let us ride along. That many more guns against any hostiles."

Cam sipped his coffee. He had arranged for a patrol of Buffalo Soldiers to escort them back, but he reckoned the army wouldn't argue too much if they were relieved of the obligation. "What's over in Menard for you and your boys, Brock?"

He scratched his bearded jaw. "Reckoned on doing some prospecting. Hear they's silver thereabouts." He sipped at his coffee.

"Afraid someone's misleading you. They're doing some mining back up at Limestone, but from what I hear, the ore doesn't assay more than an ounce or two a ton. Fellers would have to dig up a heap of rock for enough just to buy a bottle of Old Orchard at them rates."

Brock shrugged. "Probably you're right, Deputy. But we reckon on giving it a look. How about my offer?"

Cam glanced at Patch. "What are you plans?"

Patch picked at the thread holding one of the patches on the knee of his trousers. "Ain't got none. Figured I'd ride with you a spell."

Looking back at Brock, he nodded. "We'll pull out at sunrise."

Brock tossed the remainder of his coffee on the fire and scratched his head. "I still think I've seen you somewhere, Deputy." He shrugged. "Never mind. It'll come to me sooner or later."

Chapter Seven

Back at the campfire, Brock nodded to his men, who were passing around an almost empty bottle of whiskey. "We're getting closer to the pot of gold, boys. Just don't do nothing to stir things up." He took the bottle of whiskey from Lister and, to the old drunk's dismay, drained it. "Clutter. You got a good memory. What was the name of that one jasper who got away from that bank robbery down in La Grange a few months ago?"

The young outlaw frowned. "Can't remember, Brock. Let's see, seems like it was something like James—no, let's see. A funny one. Jones—no, Judson, that's it. Judson. He was the only one what the posse didn't catch up with. The others, the posse done strung up."

Curious, Hatfield scratched at the sparse patches of whiskers on his thin jaw. He frowned at Brock. "Why you asking?"

Brock shrugged. The name wasn't the same, but

the face was mighty familiar. He figured on keeping his suspicions to himself. Might have some use for them one of these days. "No reason." He rolled out his soogan and climbed between the blankets.

As one, the others followed his lead.

Milly watched as Ira and Ellie emptied their bowls of corn mush. The trip had been uneventful, despite the few assays toward her affections by the cowpokes riding guard. She had deftly handled the situation, and even though she had just learned Brock and his men were riding on to Menard with them, she was not alarmed.

Ira paused while dipping into his corn mush. "How much longer, Milly?"

She smiled warmly at her brother. "Not long. One day to Menard, then another two or so on to Limestone."

Ellie clapped her hands. "And then everything will be wonderful. We won't have to worry no more."

A look of sadness erased the smile on Milly's face. "Yes, we will, sweetheart. Until life around us changes, we'll always have to worry." She paused, then added. "We just have to be careful what we say."

Milly's warning failed to dampen Ellie's exuberance. "But, it will be wonderful. Why, you might even find you a suitor, Milly. A husband."

She laughed. "Don't count on it. It's too dangerous."

Ira frowned. "Dangerous? Why is it so dangerous?"

Growing somber, Milly explained. "Just because we don't look like our mother doesn't mean our children won't."

Ellie knitted her eyebrows, puzzled. "I don't understand. Why not?"

"Because," Milly replied, "for whatever reason the Lord made us look like Pa, is the same reason that our children might look like Ma." She arched an eyebrow. "Stop and think a minute. What are folks going to think if me or Ellie with our blond hair and fair complexions give birth to a dark-haired Indian? Or, if you, Ira, was to marry a pretty young woman, and your children came out Indian."

For several moments, the two children considered her remarks.

Ellie cleared her throat. "Does that mean we can't never get married?"

Milly smiled sadly at her sister and brother.

Cam lay staring at stars glittering in the heavens above. When Sheriff Potter had mentioned the bank robbery in La Grange, Cam's first thought was that the sheriff might suspect him. And, he still might. The payroll and the false bottom in the wagon could be a ploy to draw him out. If that was the sheriff's game, he would have a mighty long time to wait.

Rolling over on his side, Cam pulled the covers over his shoulders. He hadn't been born in the woods just to be scared by an owl. *The sheriff may or may not be playing games*, he told himself, *but I'll be ready for him one way or another.*

* * *

The small wagon train pulled out of the fort just before sunrise with the Morrison wagon in the lead. "The dust makes my daughters ill," Lydia Morrison had insisted to Cam. "They are both very delicate," she added, her tone disdainful.

Milly Barrett glanced up at Cam, then spoke to Jessica Keith. "My brother and sister and I will bring up the rear if that's all right with you, Mrs. Keith."

Jessica Keith smiled at the young woman. "That's very sweet of you, Milly. And please, call me Jessica. We've been together for two weeks now and have another to go." She shifted her feet so her back was to Lydia Morrison. "You go right ahead. When we leave Menard, I'll swap places with you. I'm used to dust," she added, cutting her eyes first toward Lydia Morrison and then rolling them.

Milly suppressed a smile. She liked Jessica Keith and her children, Penelope and Victor.

The trip to Menard proved uneventful, much to Cam's relief. Once or twice, they'd spotted figures on distant precipices watching the train. "What do you think, Cam?" Patch said, studying one of the watchers.

"Curious maybe. Or maybe weighing their chances against our firepower." He glanced over his shoulder. Sure enough, Brock and his boys were studying the distant onlookers.

Patch studied the river. "Any place along here good for an ambush?"

Casually, Cam replied, "Yep. Four or five. As we draw near, I'll ride ahead. You stay back here with Brock."

The precautions were for naught, for Cam found no sign of Comanche nor Apache during the trip to Menard. The one sign he did discover was that Patch and Penelope Keith must have had a great deal in common. Every time Cam glanced around, Patch was riding alongside the Keith wagon.

He just grinned.

Upon reaching Menard, Brock said his goodbyes and led his men to the nearest saloon. The wagons continued, stopping to camp east of town where the grass was tall and the water cold and sweet.

Cam arranged for Patch to sleep at the jail. "Just until he gets something lined up, Sheriff," Cam explained.

Potter eyed Patch shrewdly. "So you and Cam grew up together, you say?" He smoothed at his handlebar mustache idly.

Cam sensed the undertone in the sheriff's words, but it was lost on Patch. "Yes, sir. From the time we was barefoot, we was tighter than green bark on a tree. He was ornerier than a Gila monster. Went through the war together."

"And rode the grub line after that, huh?"

Patch shook his head and replied innocently. "Nope. That last fight at Bentonville separated us." He grinned at Cam. "Yesterday was the first time I seen that ugly galoot in five or six years. Like he'd dropped off the face of the earth."

The sheriff chuckled. He had learned the answer to one of his questions, but it wasn't what he wanted to learn. "Like you say, he is an ugly galoot."

They all laughed, but Cam's was edged with restraint and curiosity at the few questions the sheriff had posed to Patch.

The laughter in Sheriff Potter's eyes hid the puzzling question tumbling about in his head. Gila Monsters live in the desert, and for the most part, Arizona Territory, a territory Cam had claimed to know nothing about, that was nothing but desert.

To Cam's surprise, the three families were put up at Mrs. Garrison's boarding house, courtesy of Limestone Mines while their wagons were greased.

"Coby Asplund reckoned no one need be around when the compartment is put in and the payroll hidden." The sheriff confided in Cam.

"Which one?"

"The Barrett girl's. The wagon bed was in sad shape anyway. Coby'll tell them it needed to be repaired before it hit the trail to Limestone. It's a good enough excuse."

Just after midnight, Sheriff Potter accompanied mine superintendent Coby Asplund and mine foreman George Higgins into the barn. Asplund handed the saddlebags with the payroll to Higgins, who climbed up in the wagon.

Potter and Asplund looked on as Higgins disappeared under the wagon bonnet. They could hear the noise as the mine foreman lifted the lid to the false compartment, placed the saddlebags containing the payroll in the compartment, and refit the lid. He then slid the trunk containing the Barretts's clothing over the lid.

Asplund grinned at the sheriff. "There it is, Sheriff. Ten thousand. A lot of money."

Higgins appeared from the bonnet. Before he jumped to the ground, he gave Asplund a furtive glance. The mine superintendent nodded slyly.

The sheriff chuckled. "I reckon it'll be making a heap of them miners happy though."

They turned to leave, not one of the three having spotted the two glittering eyes watching from the loft.

Asplund and Higgins headed for the boarding house, neither looking back. From the side of his lips, Higgins said. "You got your boys ready?"

"Yep. Talbert and Hawkins. Two thousand is more than either of them jaspers ever seen."

"What about the deputy?"

"What about him? The boys will bushwhack him first. Any others if they interfere." Asplund grinned, his lips so fat they looked like they were turning inside out.

Higgins grunted. "I hope you're right."

Sweat beaded on the mine superintendent's forehead. "Not so loud. Come on to my room. We might as well make our split now."

Higgins's eyes gleamed with avarice. "Four thousand. You know, Coby, we might have stumbled on a good thing here."

The rotund man grunted. "Just stick your share under the mattress. Don't go making no big splash."

Higgins arched an eyebrow. "Don't worry about me."

Chapter Eight

The old saw that, 'two can keep a secret if one is dead,' was never more true than the night before the three families pulled out for Limestone.

Brock and two of his boys were sitting at a table in the rear of the San Saba Saloon, soaking up whiskey and laying plans for their search for Bowie's silver, when Hez Clutter quickly slipped into a chair at the table and glanced over his shoulder in the direction of the bar.

The young cowpoke leaned forward. "Now, Brock, I know you plan on getting that silver, but I just stumbled across something that might be a little faster and a heap safer than facing a passel of angry Comanches or Apaches."

Brock had grown tired of Clutter's harebrained ideas, but he had nothing better to do than listen. "What now?"

Clutter leaned closer. "Word is, the mine is sending a payroll from the bank to Limestone on one of them wagons the women is driving."

Brock stared at the younger man in disbelief, not because of the revelation of the payroll, but because when Clutter said the word, 'bank', it triggered Brock's memory of where he had seen the deputy. The deputy was the jasper pounding leather out of La Grange the day the bank was robbed. He was one of the bank robbers.

Clutter, thinking Brock's silence was his way of saying he didn't believe the young man, nodded emphatically. "It's the gospel. Heard it from that jasper, yonder at the bar. He had his back to me, but I heard him tell his partner about the payroll."

Brock followed Clutter's direction. His eyes grew wide. He shook his head. Maybe the kid wasn't harebrained. He called out. "Sundown!"

The jasper at the bar looked around. When he spotted Brock, he grinned, showing rotten teeth in a gap-toothed leer. He sauntered lazily across the smoky room, followed by another jasper, one as grizzled and cold-looking as his partner.

"Howdy, Brock. Surprised to see you up here, of all places." Sundown's cold eyes studied the men at the table with Brock.

Brock leaned back, scrutinizing the cat-eyed man in front of him. "Feeling's mutual, Sundown." He gestured to a chair. "Sit. Your pard too. Drinks are on me."

After a few minutes of hashing around old times, Brock grew serious. "Hear you boys know about a payroll going out of this here town."

Sundown shot a rattlesnake-biting look at his

partner. The lanky cowpoke held up his hands. "Not me, Sundown. I ain't said nothing."

For several moments, Sundown's hand hovered over the butt of his 44. Brock calmed the situation. "Easy, Sundown. It wasn't your boy, it was you."

Sundown gaped at him in disbelief, which quickly turned to fury. "That's a lie. Nobody heard nothing from me."

Hez Clutter stepped forward, "I did, Mister Sundown. I heard you up yonder at the bar talking to your pard about the payroll he saw them hiding in the false floor of one of them wagons that come in yesterday."

Sundown cut his eyes at Brock and snorted. "You believe this kid? A wet-behind-the-nose younker that ought to be home with his mommy?"

Brock looked up at Clutter, saw the determination in the young man's eyes, and nodded. "Yep. I reckon I do. Now," he said, shucking his six-gun and laying it on the table, "what do you got to say about that?"

Minutes later, Sundown had poured out how his partner, Blackjack, had been sleeping in the livery when the mine superintendent had been supervising the construction of a hidden compartment in the floor of the wagon. He continued watching as the carpenters left and two men came in with the sheriff. Then, one of the two stashed the ten thousand dollars in the compartment.

Brock could not contain himself. The brawny outlaw half rose from his chair. "Ten thousand?"

Sundown hushed him. In a whisper, he growled. "You want everyone else to know? Yes, blast it.

Ten thousand." He paused. "Me and Blackjack don't need nobody to help. We can do the job ourselves." His eyes narrowed. "And I won't think too kindly of anyone butting in."

From the corner of his eyes, Brock saw his men stiffening, their hands slowly dropping to the Colts. Remembering the deputy, he held out his hands to stay his men. "Maybe so, but you'd have the law after you. If you'd be willing to split the take, I got me a plan that would give us the money, and saddle the blame on a poor, dumb soul who's got no idea what's going on. We'd be away free as the birds." He studied Sundown. "Interested?"

The lanky owlhoot looked at his partner. Blackjack studied the jaspers before him, then slowly nodded. "Why not see what he's got to say? We ain't no worse off now as later."

"All right, Brock," growled Sundown, slipping into a chair at the table. "Let's see what you got to deal."

Brock nodded. "I tell you what I got to deal. I got me a jasper wanted for a bank job down in . . ." He drew up, then grinned slyly. "Never mind you where. We can put the whole blame on this old boy. While they're measuring him for a necktie, we'll be celebrating in California."

Sundown shook his head. "What happens when they catch him? He'll deny it."

With a leer on his face, Brock laughed an evil, cruel laugh. "Ain't no one going to believe him. They're going to figure since he done the bank robbery, he stole the payroll."

For several moments, Sundown considered

Brock's plan. Finally, he nodded. "All right. You're in. Now what?"

"Just be patient. And," he said, leaning forward and poking a meaty finger at them. "We don't need to be seen together." He hesitated, studying Sundown and Blackjack as well as his own men. He wrinkled his lips in disgust. None of the worthless galoots could keep their mouths shut. If he laid out his plan tonight, everyone in town would know of it by sunrise. *No*, Brock told himself, *What they don't know can't hurt nobody.* "We'll meet tomorrow night. I'll have the rest of our plans put together by then."

"Whereabouts?"

Brock shrugged. "I ain't sure." He gestured to his boys. "I think maybe me and the boys will ride up to Limestone tomorrow. You follow along behind the wagon train. I'll wangle an invite to camp with the wagon train. I'll arrange to meet you tomorrow on the road about a mile or so behind the train. I'll find you."

Sundown and Blackjack exchanged wary looks.

Brock laughed. "Don't worry, boys. I ain't going to double-cross you. You two are the most important part of my plan."

His eyes narrowing, Sundown grunted. "You best not."

"I ain't. One more thing. When you ride out, head south, then swing back around to the river."

Sundown frowned. "Why?"

Brock's black eyes flicked toward the saloon doors. "The sheriff. He's suspicious of everything. He sniffs around more than a coonhound on a hot trail. Just do what I say. Head south, then cut around."

Early next morning, Brock rode up to Cam as the rail-thin deputy was double-checking the three rigs before the ladies and their children climbed in. "Ready to pull out, huh?"

Cam nodded. "Soon as they come out," he replied, eyeing Brock's pony curiously. "You're out early."

"Yep." Brock shoved his hat to the back of his head. "Wanted to catch you before you pulled foot. Me and the boys are riding out later. Heading up around Limestone to do some prospecting like I mentioned couple nights back. Be obliged if we could camp near you folks tonight."

"Don't see no reason why not. Ladies would probably welcome the company."

Brock glanced over his shoulder to the north. "We could ride along with you on into Limestone in case of Comanche."

Cam shook his head. "Up to you. Me and Patch wouldn't turn down no help."

A crooked grin broke over the large man's bearded face. "Well, then, we'll catch up." He touched his fingers to the brim of his hat and wheeled his pony about.

As Milly gathered the remainder of her gear, she glanced out the window of the hotel. In the alley below, she saw one of Brock's men, the young one they called Clutter, talking to a grizzled hombre wearing all black. At that moment, the one in black glanced up and spotted her. A cruel grin played over his lips.

Milly jerked back from the window, and, with a shiver, hurried downstairs.

Blackjack studied the window for a moment longer, then turned back to Clutter. The dead lawman's kid. It sure was a small world.

Chapter Nine

Fifteen minutes later, with Sheriff Potter looking on, the small train splashed across the San Saba River and turned east. As usual, the Morrison wagon was in the lead, and as usual, Patch rode beside the Keith wagon, completely oblivious to the moonstruck pantomimes put on behind his back by twelve-year-old Victor Keith for the benefit of Ira Barrett in the rear wagon. Both boys were having a fine time with Patch's infatuation.

The train made almost eight miles before nooning in a small glade on the riverbank. With the help of Ira and Victor, Cam laid a communal fire, but Lydia Morrison and her daughters, Margaret and Frances, preferred one of their own.

Cam squatted at the Barrett and Keith fire for a cup of coffee. He nodded to the Morrisons. "They don't seem to like my company much," he mumbled with a half grin.

Jessica Keith laughed. "It isn't you, Deputy. They

been like that ever since we left New Braunfels."
She nodded to Milly. "We tried to be neighborly,
but Mrs. Morrison and her girls seem to prefer being
by themselves."

Ira and Victor wandered toward the river. Cam
glanced at Milly Barrett, who had spoken no more
than a few words since he met her back at Fort
McKavett. She was a handsome woman, somewhat
shy, but there was nothing wrong with that. He
cleared his throat. "Patch said you was going to
Limestone as a schoolmarm, Miss."

Milly gave her younger sister a warning look,
then cut her eyes toward Cam. "Yes."

He waited for her to continue, but when she
didn't, he commented. "You seem mighty young to
be a schoolmarm."

Milly's cheeks colored.

Ellie couldn't contain herself. "She went to the
convent."

Busying herself frying bacon and biscuits, Jessica
Keith spoke directly to the fire. "I didn't know they
had a convent in New Braunfels."

"Oh, no," replied Ellie. "It was in San Antonio.
She—"

A sharp glance from Milly cut her off. "She
means Gonzales, Mrs. Keith."

"Now, Milly," the older woman chided. "I told
you to call me Jessica."

Milly nodded. "All right, Jessica."

During the rest of the meal, Mrs. Keith kept up
a spirited conversation, sprinkled with laugher and
questions. Patch cast furtive glances at a blushing
Penelope, who sat demurely beside her mother.

Cam made no comment, but he noticed that Milly and Ellie Barrett remained unnaturally silent, reluctantly giving, from time to time, a faint smile or a brief nod to a remark or an observation.

Victor and Ira rushed up to the fire, wanting some line for fishing poles. Cam laughed. "Wait until tonight, boys. You'll have plenty time to fish."

Just before they pushed out on the trail again, the wind switched to the north. On the horizon beyond the rugged hills, a low line of dark clouds rolled toward them. Patch pursed his lips. "Maybe some weather, Cam."

Cam shook his head. "Hope not, but I reckon you're right. Let's see what kind of time we can make."

Mid-afternoon, Sundown and Blackjack reined up, surprised to see Brock and his boys astride their ponies in the middle of the trail. "Thought we were getting together tonight?"

"Change of plans," Brock replied, hooking his knee around the saddle horn and pulling out a bag of Bull Durham. "Here's what I got in mind." He gestured to the thin-jawed cowpoke at his side. "Me and Hatfield will ride in to the wagons. The rest of you hang back. I'll tell them Lister and Clutter decided against prospecting and headed north to Kickapoo Springs." He looked at the latter two. "One of them two boys, the Keith and Barrett boys, will most likely be wrangling in the morning. Sometime before sunup, Lister, you and Clutter grab him. Wear a mask. Grab him, and take him about half-an-hour away, then drop him off."

Lister said nothing, just stared at Brock. Clutter grinned evilly. Brock set his jaw and narrowed his eyes. "The boy gets hurt, I'll take care of you myself. Understand?"

The grin faded from Clutter's face. He nodded briefly.

Brock turned to Sundown and Blackjack. "You said the payroll is in the Barrett wagon, didn't you?" He directed the question to Blackjack.

"Yeah."

"She's the blond-haired woman, the one with a brother and sister."

Clutter's eyes gleamed. "What about taking her instead of the boy?"

Brock's voice was hard as granite. "Touch her, and I'll put you so full of lead you can't walk downhill."

Sundown spoke up. "What about that deputy and his sidekick?"

For a moment, Brock stared at his old friend in disgust for not catching his drift. "Why do you think I'm having these two snatch one of the boys? The deputy and his sidekick is bound to follow. When they're gone after the boy, you go in and get the payroll."

Sundown sneered. "Why don't we just shoot them?"

Brock shook his head in frustration. "Because the law don't stop chasing you for a killing. They do for a robbery. Understand now?"

Like the rising sun, the light of comprehension filled Sundown's face. He grinned crookedly at Blackjack. "Yeah. I got you."

Hez Clutter growled and patted his sidearm. "I still don't see why we just don't shoot them."

"Because, if you do, you knot-headed shavetail, I'll shoot *you*. Besides, the deputy is the one who is going to take the blame."

"What?" The young owlhoot exclaimed.

Brock nodded. "You heard me. You remember when we was riding into La Grange last summer and that cowpoke almost run over us?"

Clutter and Hatfield nodded. Charley Lister just shrugged.

Brock snorted. "Well, it was him. I thought he looked familiar. He's going by the name of Cameron, but he's really the one named Judson, the bank robber that got away." He paused. "You see what I mean about him taking the blame?"

Hatfield wrinkled his forehead in concentration. "But, how will they know he did it?"

"That's what I'm going to tell you. Pay attention. Especially you and Blackjack, Sundown. This is just as important as getting the payroll."

"What do you mean?"

Brock leaned forward, and with a leer on his square face, explained. "You got to let the women hear that Cameron and Patch set the robbery up."

"Cameron and Patch?" Sundown frowned.

"The deputy and his sidekick."

Sundown and Blackjack exchanged confused looks. "I don't understand," Sundown replied. "What good will that do?"

Brock held his temper. Patiently, he explained so even a six-year-old could understand. "When them women hear you say something like 'Cameron sure knew what he was doing' or 'Patch was right', then they'll pass word along to the law. The poor galoot won't have a chance, and we'll be free as a bird."

Sundown nodded slowly. "That's pretty smart, Brock. Pretty smart."

With a smirk, Brock grunted. He studied the faces before him. "Ever'one understand?"

They all nodded.

"All right. Me and Hatfield will ride on in, tell the deputy we decided not to stay the night, and ride out. Clutter, you and old Lister grab one of the kids just before sunup. Haul him off and leave him. Sundown, you and Blackjack hide and watch the camp. When the deputy and Patch ride out, you go in. Tomorrow at noon, we'll all meet right back here." He eyed Sundown and Blackjack narrowly. "To split the money." He studied them a moment longer, then wheeled his pony about. "Let's go, Hatfield."

The wind gusted as the two owlhoots rode east. Hatfield turned to Brock. "I don't trust them two."

Brock glanced sidelong at him. "Sundown and Blackjack?"

"Yep."

"Me neither."

A frown furrowed Hatfield's forehead. Surprised, he said. "You don't?"

"Nope. That's why after we leave the train, we ain't riding toward Limestone."

Still puzzled, Hatfield frowned again. "We ain't?"

"Nope. We'll swing around and find us a spot where we can watch the whole thing."

Hatfield thought for a moment, then grinned. "Yeah. Hey, that's right slick, Brock. Right slick."

The two hombres caught up with the wagon train an hour before sundown. Back to the north, the sky had grown dark with thick, heavy clouds. The wind, which had been coming in sporadic gusts, blew steadily now.

Cam nodded, looking past Brock and Hatfield. "Where's your boys?" Tugging his John B. down on his head against the wind, Patch rode up to join them.

With a disarming grin, Brock replied. "Decided prospecting ain't their cup of tea. Heading for Kickapoo Springs." He glanced over his shoulder at the approaching weather. "Looks like an uncomfortable night ahead." A gust of wind struck. Brock grabbed his hat to keep it from flying off.

Patch shook his head. "We'll throw up a couple canvas flies and a big fire; we'll make out."

"Yep. Reckon you will," Brock said. He nodded to Hatfield. "Appreciate your offer of letting us camp here with you, but we're riding on. Try to reach Limestone tonight."

"You'll get wet," Cam observed wryly. "You're welcome to stay. Like Patch said, we'll stay dry for the most part and warm, the rest."

Brock glanced at the horses. "Don't reckon you need to worry about them ponies tonight. Them two younkers you have did a mighty fine job of wrangling on the way up from New Braunfels, didn't they, Patch?"

With a brief nod, Patch agreed. "For boys."

With a click of his tongue, Brock urged his pony forward. "So long, boys. Take care. I'll buy the drinks when you hit Limestone."

Cam and Patch watched as the two rode on to the east. "Kind of wish he'd spent the night," Cam muttered.

Patch frowned at him. "I don't care for the man. Something sneaky about him."

"Me neither. I'd just rest easier if I could keep my eyes on him."

Patch chuckled. "I won't argue that." He looked around at Cam, who still watched after Brock and Hatfield. "What is it?"

Cam looked at his old friend thoughtfully. "What do you think he mentioned the boys for?"

Chapter Ten

They found a sheltered clearing for the night under a limestone shelf and parked the wagons end-to-end in a semi-circle facing the layered walls of limestone. To the east of the thicket was another small clearing around which Cam put Ira and Victor, stringing ropes to contain the horses.

As the boys drove the horses into the rope corral, the ladies laid a fire. Cam and Patch strung canvas flies from the ground, draped them over the wagons, and tied them securely to cedars on the overhanging ledge, building a relatively dry shelter against the expected storm.

The limestone rock would reflect the heat of the fire, making the shelter snug and cozy. Cam paused in stringing up the last fly when Lydia Morrison came up and inquired about her fire. "We always have one of our own," she said. "But there's no room in here. Can't we find another place to camp?"

Patiently, he explained there was no time because

a storm was due to hit at any moment, and besides, the horses were already corralled. "Just one night, Mrs. Morrison. That's all I ask."

If looks could kill, Cam would have been dead five times over. He glanced at Patch, who wore a silly grin. "What's bothering you?" He snapped as Mrs. Morrison stormed away.

"Nothing." Patch shrugged. "I put up with that for two weeks. You only got one night."

Within an hour, the storm struck, a blue norther howling in from the Artic, quickly dropping the temperatures. Cam dug out his heavy Mackinaw coat.

Reluctantly, the Morrisons prepared their meal at the fire with the others, then hastily retired to their wagon, preferring to keep their own company.

Jessica Keith kept a sharp eye on Patch and Penelope, who sat on a wagon tongue, laughing and giggling softly. Milly and Ellie sat beside each other, as usual saying little. The two boys were excited by the responsibility of wrangling the horses. Every ten minutes, one or the other of the boys would slip into his coat, don his oilskin slicker, and suggest to Cam that the horses might need looking after.

Cam couldn't resist grinning when he remembered himself at that age and all the exciting prospects the world held for him. That was a long time back, back when he was young and innocent and not saddled with the problems now facing him.

Cam poured himself a cup of coffee and rolled a cigarette, anticipating a lazy evening in front of a warm fire while the wind howled outside. He stared at the fire, wondering if he should attempt to strike up a conversation with Milly. He glanced at her, and she quickly looked away.

He hesitated, then decided to just keep quiet. He leaned back against a wagon wheel and touched a match to a cigarette, when he heard a cry from outside.

Cam glanced quickly at the others. No one other than Milly gave any indication of having heard. She stared at him, a tiny frown on her forehead. He held his fingers to his lips.

The cry came again.

This time, Patch heard.

Cam flicked his cigarette into the fire and motioned Patch to shuck his six-gun and skirt one end of the wagons while he went around the other end. He paused and looked at the others, signaled for them to remain silent, then slipped into the night.

The wind howled, and the rain came in sheets, but the scrub oak thicket just beyond the wagons broke much of the elements' power. Crouching against the rear wheel of the wagon, Cam peered into the night.

Then he heard the sound again, off to his left, a weak, straining cry. He eased through the thicket, staying outside the light cast from the fire. Minutes passed. All he heard was the shriek of the wind and pounding of the rain. Had it been his imagination? Or just an animal? He shivered. The wind and rain had driven the chill to the marrow of his bones.

The wind let, the rain slacked, and a soft moan came from the shadows at his feet.

Cam jumped back and squinted into the darkness. Moving slowly, he eased sideways until he could get the object between him and the fire. From time to time, the wind swayed the underbrush, moving the leaves, permitting splinters of firelight to fall across the ground.

He made out the figure of a man, a small man. He knelt and touched the man's throat. He was an old man, for the thin, wrinkled flesh hung loosely from his neck. Quickly, Cam felt for weapons. There was only a knife in a beaded sheath and a bag around the old man's neck. The old man was Indian.

Holstering his six-gun, Cam slipped his hands under the limp man's arms and dragged him back to camp.

"Who is it?" Lydia Morrison exclaimed as Cam pulled the Indian into the firelight.

"Is he dead?" Jessica Keith stepped forward tentatively.

"Just about," Cam replied, lowering him to the ground beside the fire. He studied the old man, who was wrinkled as plowed ground, skinny as a mesquite post.

"An Indian," exclaimed Margaret Morrison.

"Heaven help us," her sister screamed.

"Hush, girls," Jessica Keith ordered. "He's an old man."

Penelope Keith looked up at Patch in alarm. He shook his head. "He ain't going to hurt nobody," he assured her.

Cam knelt beside the old Indian and laid his hand on the man's chest, feeling the faint pounding of the old warrior's heart. "Get him something warm to drink."

For a moment, no one moved, then Milly quickly knelt at the fire and poured a cup of coffee. Cam took it. His eyes met hers, and he nodded. "Thanks."

She blushed.

Tilting the old Indian's head forward, Cam touched the lip of the cup to his thin lips. Feeling the warmth, the old man grabbed the cup and tried to drink it all at once. Cam held him back. "Hold on, old timer. You'll burn yourself."

Slowly, the Indian loosened his grip, permitting Cam to dole out the hot coffee. Without taking his eyes off the old man, Cam said. "He's soaked. He needs some blankets."

"Not any of mine," Lydia Morrison spat out, her voice seething with bilious hate. "Never get that Indian stench off them."

Jessica hesitated, uncertain.

Milly nodded to Ellie. "Get two of our best blankets. Heavy ones. He's cold."

When the blankets came, Cam said. "All right, ladies. Turn your heads. Me and Patch got to shuck the old man's duds."

With a shocked gasp, Mrs. Morrison led her daughters back to their wagon. Cam winked at Patch, and they quickly peeled the old Indian's buckskins from his thin frame.

Within minutes, the old man had fallen into a sound slumber, wrapped in blankets to the neck. Cam glanced from under his eyebrows at Milly, surprised and puzzled at her unhesitating offer to help an Indian. To look at her, blond-haired, fair-complexioned, he'd've guessed her to be an Injun Hater like Lydia Morrison and her spoiled daughters. "He's sleeping now."

Saying nothing, Milly glanced at him and nodded briefly.

Cam continued. "It was mighty nice of you to offer the blankets. The old man doesn't have much meat on his bones. He could have picked up a bad chill."

She smiled weakly. "He needed help. It was the Christian thing to do."

With a wry edge to his words, Cam replied. "Maybe so, but there aren't too many white Christians who would do what you did."

Milly's cheeks colored. She nodded briefly and turned to her sister. "Time for bed. You too, Ira."

The young boy made a face. "Aw, sis. Let me sleep down here with Victor. We got to take turns looking after the horses tonight." He looked hopefully at Cam. "Ain't that right, Cam?"

Cam grinned up at Milly. "If your sister don't mind."

For a moment, Milly pondered her answer, then gave a brief nod. "Just stay dry, you hear?"

Ira's face broke into a broad smile. "Don't worry, sis. I will."

After everyone had settled in for the night, Cam poured himself another cup of six-shooter coffee and rolled a cigarette. Outside, the wind howled. He considering staying put the next day if the wind continued. Sharp as it was, it could drive a chill into a body that made it seem twenty degrees colder. With a sigh, he stretched and decided to wait and see what the morning brought.

With a chuckle, he told himself that the trip so far had been mighty interesting. "I reckon it would have to go some to get any more interesting," he muttered, completely unaware of just how prophetic his words were.

Chapter Eleven

Three hundred yards to the south, Sundown and the others sprawled around a roaring fire in a large cave, passing a bottle around. Theirs would be a warm and snug night.

A voice from the night electrified them. "Hello."

Instantly alert, the owlhoots shucked their six-guns.

"Drifters, boys. Saw your fire," the voice called out. "Just two of us."

Blackjack shrugged at Sundown. "Come on in, but with your hands high."

Two trail-worn cowpokes came into the firelight. "Howdy." The first one nodded. "Name's Hawkins. This here feller behind me is Talbert. We's heading for Limestone. Sure would appreciate sharing the cave with you old boys."

Sundown studied them a moment, quickly realizing that once word of the robbery spread around the countryside, these two would remember seeing

Sundown and the others. Wouldn't do much good to put the blame on that deputy only to have these two turn them into the sheriff. "Come in and squat. Make yourself at home." He glanced at Blackjack, who lifted an eyebrow. Sundown nodded.

"Yep," Blackjack drawled, holstering his six-gun. "We're all friends here."

That night, while Hawkins and Talbert slept, Sundown put a bullet in their temples.

Another few hundred yards distant, Brock and Hatfield huddled miserably around a small fire beneath a rocky ledge, holding their collars tight around their necks. Brock cursed to himself, figuring that he deserved the lion's share of the plunder for the discomfort forced upon him by the storm.

During the early morning hours, the wind lessened, and the rain slacked off. Cam stepped outside to study the conditions. He decided they should push on. The temperature remained chilly, but Cam knew that without the biting wind piercing a body's clothing, the heat generated by the exertion from riding would help maintain warmth.

True to their word, the boys had taken regular turns checking on the horses throughout the night. Unknown to them, however, Cam awakened each time one left and remained awake until the boy returned.

Early that same morning, Charley Lister and Hez Clutter reluctantly rolled out of their soogans and saddled their ponies. As they rode from the cave, their horses shied at the two bodies lying in the mud outside the mouth of the cave.

"I don't know about you," Clutter whispered. "But I'm mighty glad to get away from that there Sundown and Blackjack fellers. They raise the hackles on my neck."

Lister grunted. "My feelings in spades."

Leaving their horses tied in a patch of scrub oak north of the corralled horses, the two owlhoots found a nook out of the cold only a few feet from the trail along which the boy would travel from the wagons to the horses.

They removed their hats, slipped masks over their heads, then tugged their hats back down on their heads. "Remember," whispered Lister. "You grab him and clamp your hand over his mouth. I'll gag him right fast."

Clutter nodded. "Be easier to whop him across the head," the younger man muttered.

Lister grunted. "You do it, and Brock'll whop you across the head."

Inside the shelter, Cam awakened. He glanced around, expecting to see one of the boys sliding into his oilskin, but both lay sleeping the sleep of the dead. With a grin, he slipped on his heavy coat and oilskin and tugged his hat on his head. *Let the boys sleep*, he told himself, ducking his head as he stepped under the fly into the early morning darkness.

* * *

"Get ready," whispered Lister when they heard the feet slogging through the mud. "Here comes one."

Clutter eased into a crouch, ready to leap. At his side, Lister unrolled the gag for the boy's mouth. A figure came around the bend in the trail. Both men froze and held their breaths as the dark figure trudged past, shoulders hunched against the cold.

After he disappeared among the trees, the two men eased back into the darkness of their tiny nook. Moments later, the figure returned. When he drew even with their hiding place, he paused. He appeared as only a vague shadow in the night, but Lister shivered. He had the feeling that whoever the jasper was, he was staring straight at them.

After what seemed like hours, the hombre continued on his way.

"Wonder what's gone wrong?" Clutter whispered, speculation edging his words.

Lister hissed. "Ain't nothing gone wrong. Just you wait and see."

Victor Keith had awakened upon Cam's return. He grimaced. "I didn't mean to oversleep," he exclaimed apologetically.

Cam chuckled. "Don't worry about it, boy. You can check next time." He pulled the blankets over his shoulders, grinning to himself, knowing full well the youngster wouldn't sleep a wink until his turn to check the horses.

Thirty minutes later, Cam watched as Victor pushed the fly aside and headed for the horses. Rolling his shoulders, he sat up, figuring it was time to build up the fire and put on the coffee.

After tossing a few logs on the fire, Cam saw the old Indian was awake. He grabbed the Indian buckskins from the wagon wheel where they had dried and handed them to the old man whose black eyes were staring up at him. Cam gave the old man a crooked grin. "You speak white man talk?"

The old man nodded as he slipped into his buckskins.

Cam reassured the old man he had nothing to fear. "You can ride along with us, or if you decide to stay here, we'll give you what grub we can spare."

Without a word, the old man nodded again.

"What do they call you?" Cam pointed to him, then touched his finger to his own chest. "They call me Cam."

The old warrior nodded. "Me Blue Stick. Me Comanche."

"Your people leave you to die?"

Blue Stick gave a single nod.

Cam grinned again. "You don't look like you're ready to die."

"Me not." Blue Stick shook his head.

At that moment, Patch rolled out of his soogan and stomped over to the fire. Cam glanced over his shoulder. "Before you get too comfortable, go check on Victor. He should be back by now. I don't want him fooling around with those horses."

Cam turned to Blue Stick. "Once the ladies start breakfast, I reckon it'll be a heap busy around the fire," he said, knowing the old Indian probably had no idea what he was saying. He picked up the blankets and spread them by the wagon wheel. "You'll be out of the way over here."

A few minutes later, Patch returned.

Cam paused before placing another log on the fire. "Where's the boy?"

Patch looked around. "He wasn't out there. I figured he was back here."

A gasp behind him jerked Cam around. Jessica Keith stood staring at him in disbelief, her fisted hands pressed against her lips. Beside her, Penelope stared at Patch.

Cam gave Patch a warning glance, then turned to Jessica. "Nothing to be alarmed about. The boy's probably climbing a tree or following a deer. I'll go see. Just don't you worry yourself none." It was a lie, and it was a poor lie.

By now, the others had climbed from their wagons and looked on in consternation. Patch spoke up. "Just go about breakfast. We'll have him back before the bacon's done fried up crisp," he said, buttoning his Mackinaw against the cold.

The sky had grown light, light enough so the tracks in the mud were easy to see. On the other hand, Cam realized, the trail had been traveled several times since the rain ceased, which made the specific sign difficult to read.

Victor was not to be found at the corral. In fact, it appeared the last tracks to be made around the horses were those left by Cam on his earlier visit.

Patch frowned. "Where in the Sam Hill could that youngster have gotten off to?"

"Can't figure it," Cam mumbled, scratching his head. "Let's head back up the trail. See if we can find if he went off it."

"Why would he do that?"

"Who knows what these younkers will do today. He might have heard some turkeys gobble and figured he could catch one."

Patch arched a skeptical eyebrow.

Cam shrugged. "You got a better explanation?"

"Reckon not," Patch replied with a rueful grin.

Painstakingly, they slowly made their way back toward the wagons, each studying his side of the trail. Patch jerked to a halt. "Look here. More tracks. Grown-up."

"You sure they're not ours?" Cam frowned.

"Not unless one of us has taken to wearing brogans."

Cam leaned forward. Patch was right. The imprint of the flat round heel of a brogan was plainly visible. "And take a look here," he said, pointing to a small footprint in the middle of the others. For several moments, the two studied the sign, following it a few feet until the small prints vanished.

Cam looked up at Patch in disbelief.

Patch gave his head a single shake. "It don't make sense to me. Why would somebody carry the boy off?"

"Makes no sense to me either," Cam replied, shouldering into the scrub oak and following the clear trail. At the edge of the oak, they found where two men had hoisted Victor on a horse with one of them and headed north.

Cam cursed, then scanned the sky. The heavy

clouds looked as if they would drop a flood at any moment. "We got to move and move fast," he blurted out, turning and racing back to the camp. "Bring our ponies to the wagons. I'll tell the women."

Quickly, Cam detailed the events indicated by the sign. Jessica Keith screamed and fainted. Penelope and Milly knelt at her side, trying to revive her. The Morrisons stood crying in front of their wagon as Cam continued. "Me and Patch are going after the boy. You folks will be fine here. Weather's too bad for any hostiles." He looked at Ira, whose face was drawn and pale. "You take care of the women, you hear?"

Milly looked up at him in alarm, fearful for her brother. Cam explained. "Time for him to grow up."

At that moment, Patch led the ponies inside the shelter. They were quickly saddled. Cam paused before mounting and turned to Milly. "We got to have somebody strong. I don't cotton to put the job on anyone, but there's no choice. You got to help your brother."

Chapter Twelve

Sundown grinned evilly at Blackjack from where they sat behind a motte of scrub oak, watching Cam and Patch ride north on the trail of the kidnappers. "Looks like old Brock knew what he was talking about," he said.

"Yep," replied Blackjack, squinting through the oak leaves at the disappearing riders. "I just hate to share that ten thousand with them old boys."

"Me too, but there's something to say for Brock's plan. I'd rather have a couple thousand for the two of us and not worry about the law than have the whole shebang and keep running. Why, we can ride into the nearest saloon and buck the tiger without worrying about the law nosing around."

As soon as Cam and Patch disappeared over the rim of a ridge, the two owlhoots headed for the wagons, completely unaware that their every step was being scrutinized by Brock and Hatfield.

* * *

Ten minutes later, with six-guns drawn and masks over their faces, Sundown and Blackjack burst through the canvas flies into the shelter. When Lydia Morrison saw the two outlaws, she promptly fainted. Her daughters were too petrified to go to her aid.

Sundown growled. "All right, ladies. Just you be quiet, and no one gets hurt." He saw Blue Stick leaning against the wagon wheel. "You too, Injun."

Blackjack spotted Ira trying to swing a rifle around toward them. In two quick strides, he ripped it from the boy's hands and slammed the youth to the ground with the back of his hand.

Milly screamed and leaped upon Blackjack, ripping his mask from his face. With a growl, he knocked her to the floor.

Jessica Keith, having recovered from her fainting spell, promptly swooned again, collapsing in her daughter's arms.

Blackjack knelt by Milly's side and hissed a warning to her. "You saw me back in Menard, but I seen you months ago down in San Antonio before your Pa died." He cut his beady eyes at the white women. "Appears you got these Christian white folks fooled. You just keep your pretty little mouth closed about me, and I'll forget that you and yours are nothing better than mangy half-breeds."

She stared at him in shock.

"You hear me?"

Slowly, she nodded.

Sundown strode to Milly and touched the muzzle of his six-gun to her shoulder. "You. Blondie. Which is your wagon?"

Stunned by Blackjack's warning, she stared blankly at Sundown.

He shifted the muzzle to Ira's chest. "I'm waiting."

She shook her head sharply, trying to gather her thoughts. "The last one. Over there."

The outlaw took a step back, his eyes on the women, and called out to Blackjack. "You hear? The last wagon. That's where Cameron said the payroll money was hidden."

Blackjack grinned at Sundown. "I'll take a look. If him and Patch was lying, I'll shoot them both."

Across the room, the two Morrison girls hugged each other while their unconscious mother lay at their feet. They jerked around in wide-eyed surprise when they heard Blackjack's threat.

Cam and Patch? Milly's eyes grew wide. She looked around at Penelope, who stared at her in disbelief from where she knelt beside her mother. They both turned back to the wagon in time to see Blackjack jump down with saddlebags in his hand.

"Here it is," he called out. "Just where Cameron and Patch said it would be."

Sundown tipped his hat. "Thank you, ladies. It's been a pleasure."

The two stepped outside and hurried up the ridge to where they had tied their ponies.

Blackjack laughed. "I still think we ought to keep it ourselves."

"Not me," Sundown replied. "I've known Brock too long. He'd track us down if it was the last thing he did."

A voice froze them just as they reached their

horses. "You're smarter than I gave you credit for, Sundown."

As one, Sundown and Blackjack looked around into the muzzle of Joe Brock's six-gun. "You just saved two lives, yours and your greedy friend's there. Now, toss me them bags."

Sundown hesitated. "What about our share?"

Brock holstered his revolver. "You'll get it, but I carry the money. Now, toss it here, and we'll head back to meet with the rest of the boys."

A mile or so to the north, Cam held up his hand and pulled his pony to a halt. "Take a look," he exclaimed.

Waving to them from across a small valley was Victor Keith. With a shout, he raced toward them. Cam studied the valley and the surrounding oak, but there was no sign of the kidnappers.

He looked at Patch, who appeared just as puzzled.

After assuring them he was unharmed, Victor swung up behind Cam for the ride back to camp. He quickly told them of the kidnapping.

"No, sir. They didn't hurt me none. Oh, the ropes burned my wrists, and the way they laid me over the saddle, the bouncing hurt my belly, but after a spell, they pulled up, dropped me to the ground, and rode away. By the time I got the blindfold off, they had disappeared."

Patch pursed his lips. "They talk or anything so you could recognize a voice?"

Victor shook his head. "Not a word. I got myself untied easy enough. They really didn't tie me all that tight."

Cam stared at the rugged country before him. A kidnapping that turned out not to be a kidnapping. Tying up a boy so he could untie himself.

Cam arched an eyebrow. "Something don't smell right."

Patch nodded. "I smell the same thing. You know, I remember once when Comanches wanted some of Pa's horses. They'd send a few bucks to shoot at the house. Get us all inside, then run off the horses over the hill." He paused. "Why would someone want us to be away from the wagons?"

Suddenly, Cam knew the answer. With a soft curse, he spurred his bay. "Hold on, boy," he called over his shoulder. "Hold on."

"Hey! What's going on?" Patch shouted.

"Somebody just pulled one of them Comanche tricks on us."

Patch dug his heels into his pony's flank. The racing animal pulled up beside Cam's bay. "What are you talking about?" Patch shouted.

Cam clenched his teeth. "You'll see."

Chapter Thirteen

After Blackjack and Sundown fled the shelter, Milly hugged Ira to her. "Are you all right?"

His reddened cheek stinging from the backhanded slap, Ira clenched his teeth in anger. "It don't hurt."

Jessica Keith moaned and managed to sit up. "W-What happened?"

Penelope and Milly exchanged looks filled with unanswered questions. Neither young woman voiced their alarm. Penelope knelt by her mother. "It's all right, mother. They're gone."

The older woman suddenly became alert. She looked around the shelter. "My boy. Where's my boy?"

Ira slipped outside with a Winchester as Milly hurried to her. "Cam and Patch are looking for him, Jessica. He'll be all right. I'm positive."

Margaret Morrison's shrill voice cut through the cold air. "Don't believe her, Mrs. Keith. Patch and

88

Cam are the ones who told the robbers where the payroll was."

Penelope frowned at Milly. "It was in your wagon. Didn't you know about it?"

Frances Morrison arched an eyebrow and crossed her arms over her breast. Her tone condemning, she declared. "She had to know about it."

"No," shouted Milly. "I had no idea it was there."

Her voice strident, Margaret demanded. "Then how did it get there?"

Milly shook her head. "I don't know. Wait a minute. The night the sheriff put us up at the hotel. You remember. They wanted to grease the axles and hubs. That's when they did it. That was the only time they could have hidden the payroll."

By now, Jessica Keith had struggled weakly to her feet. Penelope put her arm around her mother's shoulder and led her to the fire.

"A likely story," Frances Morrison said. She jabbed a bony finger at Blue Stick, who remained wrapped in a blanket and leaning against a wagon wheel. "For all we know, he's part of it."

"No," Milly shouted.

Margaret narrowed her eyes. "What did that outlaw say to you?"

Milly hesitated.

Margaret insisted. "He said something. What was it?"

"Nothing." Milly shook her head. "He wanted to know which wagon was mine. That was all."

At that moment, Ira burst in. "Milly! Look who's here. The army."

Right on his heels, a young lieutenant followed by a sergeant and two privates stepped around the end of the wagons.

Cries of relief filled the shelter, and everyone except Milly tried to tell her own story at the same time, futile efforts that succeeded in making the confusion all the more palpable.

"Hold it, hold it," shouted the lieutenant, raising his arms. "One at a time, ladies. One at a time." When they grew silent, he continued. "I'm Lieutenant Brooks. This is Sergeant O'Malley and Privates Wilson and Melder. We've out of Fort McKavett." He spotted Blue Stick. His eyes grew cold. He nodded to the sergeant and gestured to the old Indian. "Now, ladies," he said. "The boy here says you were robbed. Someone want to tell me what happened?"

They all started talking once again.

"Wait a minute, wait a minute. One at a time," shouted the lieutenant over the commotion. "You, ma'am," he said to Lydia Morrison. "Why don't you tell me what took place here?"

She wrung her hands. "All I saw was two dirty-looking men come in by the fire."

"Then what?"

"I fainted."

Behind the lieutenant, the sergeant stifled a laugh. Over his shoulder, Lieutenant Brooks growled. "That's enough, Sergeant."

"Yes, sir."

"What about you, ma'am," Brooks said to Jessica Keith.

Sheepishly, she ducked her head. "I'm afraid I fainted also, Lieutenant."

Brooks clenched his jaw, then in a tightly constrained voice said. "Is there anyone who did not faint?"

Margaret Morrison stepped forward. "I saw the whole dreadful thing, Lieutenant." She quickly detailed the events, then added, "and one of those horrid men said that Cameron and Patch had told them the payroll was hidden in her wagon." She pointed an accusing finger at Milly.

"Cameron and Patch? Who are they?"

"The deputy and his friend. They're taking us to Limestone," Milly replied. "And I didn't know the payroll was in my wagon," she added, glaring at Margaret Morrison.

"Where are they now? This Cameron and Patch."

She explained that Victor Keith had disappeared and the two were searching for him.

Frances Morrison shook her head emphatically. "Those two will never come back. We all heard those robbers. Cameron and Patch told them where the payroll was hidden."

"Did any of you recognize the robbers?"

"They had masks, Lieutenant," said Milly, hoping he couldn't hear the pounding of her heart.

"So you couldn't recognize them?"

Margaret pointed at Milly. In an accusing tone, she said, "You tore the mask off one of them."

Lieutenant Brooks looked sharply at Milly. "I thought you said they had masks, Miss."

"They did," she replied hastily. "I did tear one

off, but I didn't recognize him. I mean, I didn't know him."

"But, you could identify him now."

She nodded slowly.

He looked around. "Any of you others identify him?"

The women shook their heads.

At that moment, Victor Keith burst into the shelter. "Ma," he shouted, running to Jessica Keith. Cam and Patch followed him inside.

"That's them," screamed Margaret Morrison.

Her sister echoed her. "That's them. They're the ones who told the robbers where the payroll was hidden."

Lieutenant Brooks barked. "Sergeant!"

Three breech-loading Sharps turned on Cam and Patch, their .54 caliber muzzles looking like cannons.

"Hold on, Lieutenant," said Cam, holding his hands high. "What's going on here?"

"Your name Cameron?"

Cam nodded.

The lieutenant turned to Patch. "You're Patch?"

Patch eyed the rifles trained on them warily. "I don't think so."

"That's him. That's Patch," Margaret Morrison shouted.

The lieutenant indicated the women with a nod of his head. "These ladies say two robbers wearing masks stole a payroll from one of the wagons and claimed you two had told them where it was hidden."

For a moment, all Cam could do was stare at the

lieutenant in disbelief. "They what?" He looked at Milly.

She nodded. "Two men, dirty and mean-looking, went straight to my wagon and took the payroll from a secret panel in the floor of the wagon." She hesitated, then added softly. "They said you and Patch told them where it was hidden."

Patch's jaw dropped open. "Me? I didn't even know there was a payroll." He looked at Cam. "Cam? What the Sam Hill's going on here?"

Cam nodded and spoke to Lieutenant Brooks. "He's right, Lieutenant. Let me explain. I'm the deputy in Menard, and—."

"You won't be when the sheriff hears what you did," Lydia Morrison screamed.

Cam paused at her outburst, then continued. "Coby Asplund, the mine superintendent at Limestone, had been having his payrolls hijacked. They put the ladies up at the hotel in Menard for one night while they built a hidden compartment in the floor of Miss Barrett's wagon. Nobody out here knew about it except me. Not even Patch."

"Then why did the robbers use Patch's name?" Lieutenant Brooks eyed Patch suspiciously.

Cam shook his head. "I can't answer that one for you, Lieutenant. But, you can ask Sheriff Potter in Menard. He'll verify what I'm telling you."

"Maybe he will. Maybe he won't. Until then, you boys are my prisoners. How much was the payroll?"

"Sheriff Potter said it was ten thousand."

Sergeant O'Malley whistled.

"That's enough, Sergeant." He gestured to a young private. "Private Wilson, you ride back to

Menard and tell the sheriff the payroll has been stolen. We'll take the wagon train on to Limestone, then return to Menard with the two suspects."

The young soldier nodded, saluted, and hurried from the shelter. Brooks nodded to Cam and Patch's sidearms. "I'll have those revolvers."

Patch and Cam exchanged glances, then relinquished their handguns. The lieutenant nodded to Blue Stick. "Where did the Injun come from?"

"Found him outside last night. He's an old man. Figure his people left him to die. He's got no weapons. Just his knife."

"What are going to do with him?"

Cam glanced around at the women facing him. "I planned to ask one of the ladies to take him on into Limestone with us. Can't leave him here to die."

Brooks sneered. "I can."

"Not in my wagon," Lydia Morrison shrieked.

"He can go in mine." Milly looked up at Cam. "I'll take him into Limestone."

Cam smiled gratefully.

Jessica stepped forward. "Are you sure, Milly? He's a savage."

The word ripped at Milly's heart. She nodded stiffly. "He's a human being, and like Cam said, he's dying. He might not make it through the day, but I'll be able to sleep at night knowing I did what I thought was the decent thing to do."

Lydia Morrison spun on her heel. "Well," she exclaimed. "And a white woman at that."

Chapter Fourteen

With Blue Stick in the rear of the wagon, Milly reined her team in behind the Keith wagon, her thoughts more on her own predicament than what lay ahead at the end of the journey. She couldn't help wondering if Joe Brock was somehow involved in the robbery. From her hotel window, she had seen the robber she had unmasked palavering with Hez Clutter, one of Brock's men. But, if she told the law, then the outlaw would reveal the secret she was so desperately trying to keep. She muttered a silent prayer.

"Milly? Hey, Milly?"

Ira's voice jerked her from her thoughts. "What?"

"You think Cam and Patch are outlaws like the Morrisons say?"

She sighed deeply. "I don't want to think so. Penelope thinks the world of Patch."

"Don't you like Cam some, huh?"

She felt her ears burn. "Hush up, Ira."

"Well, I've seen the way you look at him when he ain't looking."

Her cheeks grew hot. She glared down at him. "I said you hush up now. You hear?"

He laughed. "I've seen you. You just won't admit it."

She jerked her head around, eyes forward. "Makes no difference. I told you before. Makes no difference what I think about anybody. You neither. None of us can take a chance on something going wrong."

"I sure would like to get my hands on those robbers. You think the law will put some kind of reward on them?"

"I don't know. You just forget about them," she snapped. "The less you know, the better off you are."

Undaunted by her sharp reprimand, the excited young boy exclaimed. "Not me. We could sure use some of that reward money."

She snapped at him again. "Now, you listen to me, Ira Barrett. I don't want you talking about those robbers anymore, you hear? Not another word."

He frowned at her, surprised at the vehemence in her tone. "What's wrong, sis?"

"Nothing." She stared straight ahead.

"Yes, there is. You never talk hateful like that. Something's wrong."

She knew she should say nothing, but she felt compelled to get her feelings off her chest. "Because, Ira. I recognized the man who robbed us. And I think I know who he works for."

"You do? What's his name?"

"I don't mean that," she replied in a low voice. "I saw him back in Menard. I think I know who he works for."

Ira glanced toward Lieutenant Brooks at the head of the train. "Why didn't you tell the lieutenant?"

Milly gave him a wry laugh. "It isn't that easy, little brother. I don't know how, but the outlaw knows us. He knows about us from San Antonio. He knows all about us."

The young boy studied her a moment, letting her words soak in. His forehead knit in a frown. "What do you mean, he knows all about us?"

Milly remained silent, her eyes on the road ahead.

"You mean," Ira began tentatively. "You mean he knows about us? He really does?"

She cut her eyes sharply at him. "And if we say a word, he'll tell everyone. And you know what that means. We'd have to move again. Maybe keep on moving."

Ira sat back in the seat. "You think he'll keep his promise if you don't say nothing?"

Milly arched an eyebrow. "That's what I'm counting on. I'm tired of running. I want to settle someplace and not have to worry about someone finding out about us."

"Me too."

They fell silent, each lost in his own thoughts. Once, Milly glanced sidelong at her brother, a faint smile playing over her lips as she wistfully remembered her brother's assertion that she had paid Cam more attention that she would admit.

* * *

Joe Brock's eyes grew cold, and the muscles in his rock-like jaw writhed like snakes as he peered inside the saddlebags. He glared murderously at Sundown and Blackjack.

Puzzled, Sundown and Blackjack looked at each other, then back at Brock, who had retrieved the few packs of greenbacks and was holding them in his left hand, his right dropping to the butt of his six-gun. His eyes grew hard. "You just made the worst mistake in your life, Sundown."

Sundown frowned. "What the Sam Hill you talking about, Brock? You act like you got some bad whiskey."

Brock's men stiffened at the accusation in their boss's words. They turned their eyes on the two newcomers warily. Brock kept his cold, black eyes fixed on Sundown and Blackjack as he spoke over his shoulder to his men. "There's only two thousand here, Boys. The payroll was ten thousand."

He paused. His men muttered threats.

Sundown's eyes grew wide, then quickly narrowed as he realized what Brock was insinuating. His gaze flicked to Brock's hand on the butt of his six-gun. Slowly, he extended his hands to the side in a show of non-violence. "Now, take it easy, Brock. Don't do nothing until we talk."

"Talk?" Brock snorted. "We'll talk when one of you jaspers pulls the other eight thousand from under your shirt, and then the two of you ride out."

In a calm, patient voice, Sundown said. "Hold on, now, Brock. We ain't that stupid. Everyone knowed there was ten thousand in them bags. Ain't no way we'd try to steal from you old boys."

Brock's eyes narrowed. "I ain't saying it again. Fork over that eight thousand."

Taking a deep breath and slowly releasing it, Sundown replied. "All right, Brock. If there's only two thousand there, I can see how you figure one of us hid it on the way up the hill to the horses. We been with you since then. If we hid it on us, we ain't had time to get rid of it. All you boys got to do is search us. You'll see we ain't got it."

"Nobody's searching me," Blackjack growled.

The roar of a six-gun obliterated Blackjack's words. He never felt the slug that caught him in the middle of his forehead and sent him tumbling off the back of his horse.

With a curse, Sundown grabbed for his revolver, but three slugs tore him from the saddle. He was dead before he hit the ground.

"Get down there and search them," Brock ordered. "Get the rest of the payroll."

Young Hez Clutter jumped to the ground and quickly searched the bodies. He frowned up at Brock. "They ain't got it on them, Brock."

Brock's face darkened. Clutter took a step back, his eyes filled with fear. "Lister," Brock hissed. "You look."

The old man pulled out his knife and ripped open shirts and trousers, then pulled off the boots. He looked up and shook his head and nodded to the near naked bodies. "They ain't hiding nothing, Brock. Not even a tick."

Brock cursed.

Hatfield spoke up. "We saw them come out from under the canvas, Brock. The only time we couldn't see them was when they went behind that ledge, and they was out of sight no longer than a jasper could blink. You reckon they hid it there?"

Brock glared at Hatfield, then shook his head. "Let's find out." But, in the back of his mind, he wondered. Eight thousand missing. Hatfield was right. The two hadn't been out of sight long enough to hide anything. All they would have had time to do was toss the greenbacks in some weeds or tall grass. He frowned. "Hold on," he muttered to himself. "Why would they have even done that? They had no idea me and Hatfield was waiting for them."

"What about them?" Hatfield nodded to the bodies sprawled in the road.

With a grunt, Brock replied. "Drag them into the bushes."

"What about their horses?"

"You want to fool with them, sell them or shoot them."

Heavy clouds covered the sun, and the air carried a chill as the wagon train rumbled along beside the San Saba River. Cam and Patch rode at the head of the train with Lieutenant Brooks on one side and Sergeant O'Malley behind, his breech loading Sharps laying across his lap.

There were few words spoken. Each was absorbed with his own thoughts. The lieutenant had a single goal in mind, to get the train safely to Limestone, then escort the two thieves back to Menard. Sergeant O'Malley was eagerly anticipating a visit to the local saloon in Limestone. Patch was still trying to figure out how he had gotten into such a mess. And Cam knew that if he rode into Limestone with the cavalry, his next stop was the jail and then a lynching at La Grange.

A voice from behind called to the lieutenant. It was Lydia Morrison, demanding they stop for a noon break. Brooks agreed, and a few minutes later, fires blazed and noon dinner fried in the skillets.

Patch and Cam tended the horses under the watchful eyes of Private Melder, who had plopped down on a small boulder several feet away.

"Cam, what the blazes is going on here?" Patch whispered as he lifted a horse's front hoof as if checking for rocks.

Cam did the same with another horse. "No idea. The payroll was the idea of Coby Asplund. Him and some guy named Higgins were the one who had the hidden compartment built and hid the money inside. Sheriff Potter watched them."

"How much did you say the payroll was, ten thousand?"

"Ten thousand is what the sheriff said."

Patch whistled softly. He dropped the foot, then brushed at the horse's mane. "The sheriff will straighten it out, you reckon?"

Cam chuckled bitterly. "For you, but not for me."

"What do you mean?" Patch frowned.

Moving in front of the horse and making a pretense of adjusting the bridle and bit, Cam explained. "I told you about the bank in La Grange. Well, I figure that once the army gets me back to Menard and starts checking, they'll find out the truth." He cut his eyes to Patch. "I've got to make a break before then. If I don't find out who stole the payroll before the army or the sheriff starts checking on me, I'll be staring up at six feet of dirt courtesy of the hangman's rope."

Patch's eyes met Cam's. "Tell me what to do."

Stepping back from the horse, Cam scratched the animal's forehead, all the while under the watchful eye of Private Melder. "Nothing. I don't want you to take a hand. Just stay out of the way. I don't want them to say you were part of it."

Chapter Fifteen

Brock and his boys scoured the trail from the camp to the ridge and then up the hill. There was no sign of the eight thousand, no convenient nooks or crannies where the greenbacks could have been hastily secreted, no stack of rocks or patches of weeds concealing it.

Young Clutter looked around at Brock. "I reckon them two was telling us the truth, huh?"

With a grimace, Brock grunted. "They shouldn't of drawed on us then." With a click of his tongue, he rode his horse under the rocky shelf where the train had camped the night before. "Come on in, boys. Might as well divvy up what we got."

Clutter grinned like a possum. Yes, sir, he had his celebration already planned out. He still remembered that young woman with strawberry blonde hair at Miss Dora's down in Cherry Springs in Gillespie County. He reckoned he would really show her a bang-up time with his share of the loot.

Sheriff Potter stared up at Private Wilson, digesting the implications of the message the young soldier had delivered. Had he misjudged Cam? And had he made a mistake by not acting upon the information in the letter Cam had brought from Mason? He didn't think so. The description sent by the sheriff of La Grange could fit a thousand cowpokes, Cam included. No, he told himself. He had not made a mistake. He rose and ordered the young man to accompany him. "Across the street," he explained. "Limestone Mine Headquarters."

Inside, Coby Asplund listened in mock horror and feigned anger as the young soldier repeated the message. The rotund mine superintendent turned his eyes angrily on Sheriff Potter. "Ten thousand dollars," he exclaimed. "Ten thousand."

Potter shook his head. "Someone had to know about it."

Asplund sputtered. "Who? Only you, me, and George Higgins knew the payroll was hid in that false compartment."

"No. We weren't the only ones," Sheriff Potter replied. "My deputy, Cameron, knew."

"Your deputy?" Asplund's shock was genuine. For a moment, he thought perhaps his plan had gone astray, that another had stolen the payroll. Then he realized it made no difference. The payroll had been hijacked, and he was home free. "Why in the Sam Hill did you do that, Sheriff?"

"He had to know," Sheriff Potter replied. "Anything that valuable, he had to know. I trust the man, Mister Asplund. He ain't the kind to turn bad."

The mine superintendent demanded. "Who is this deputy? I want him investigated." Asplund smiled inwardly at his last remark. He couldn't have asked for a more accommodating scenario even if he had designed it himself.

"I told you. His name's Cameron. Good man."

"I demand you put together a posse immediately. I'll put up a reward of two thousand dollars. I want those outlaws caught and prosecuted."

"Easy, easy. I'll ride out and take a look around. No sense in two dozen horses wiping out any sign that might be there."

"Of course, Sheriff. You're right. You're right. I didn't mean to be so blunt. It's just that I'm worried about all those miners with no pay." He shook his head and, he hoped with the right touch of compassion, added. "Many of those hard working boys up there are mighty hard up."

"Beg your pardon, Sheriff," interrupted the young private. "According to the ladies, a man named Cameron and Patch told the robbers where the payroll was hidden."

Potter was momentarily stunned.

Asplund caught his breath, confused by the sudden turn. Hastily, he collected his thoughts and reminded himself that it made no difference who stole the money. No one would believe a thief's word against a leading businessman's. "Cameron? Didn't you say he was your deputy, Sheriff?"

The sheriff nodded slowly.

"And you say he knew where the payroll was hidden?"

"Yep. I reckon he did." Resignation hung heavy in his voice. He couldn't believe what he had heard, yet, the young soldier nor the ladies had no reason to lie.

Asplund drew up his shoulders. "Well, Sheriff, it looks to me that you got a deputy turned outlaw to run down."

With a drawn-out sigh of frustration, Potter nodded. "I reckon I do."

Asplund watched through the front window as the sheriff crossed the street. How in the blazes did Cameron and Patch get involved in the robbery? Hawkins and Talbert were the outsiders he'd brought in. They couldn't have known the deputy or his friend. Unless, the sly mine superintendent told himself, they learned the deputy's name and repeated it in front of the ladies to throw the law off their own trail.

He considered the possibility. "No," he muttered to the dingy window after a few moments. "Neither of them jaspers is that smart." With a frown wrinkling his forehead, he stared blankly out the window, trying to figure out what had happened. On the other hand, he told himself once again, it made no difference. The payroll was gone. A crooked grin played over his face. Four thousand in his pocket, and that bad-luck deputy out there taking the blame. Life couldn't be better.

* * *

Mid-afternoon, the wagon train hit Calf Creek and turned north. "Another three or four miles," Lieutenant Brooks commented. "We'll spend the night in Limestone and start back before sunrise."

Patch and Cam glanced at each other. The narrow road twisted over and around limestone ledges and granite upthrusts, up and down gullies and washes as it continued to roughly parallel Calf Creek on their right. Though Cam was unfamiliar with the country, he knew he had to make his break soon. He just hoped he didn't run into a box canyon or off a bluff.

Lydia Morrison gave him the chance he needed.

As they rounded a bend and dropped down a slight incline, she reined up and called out. "Lieutenant! We have to stop."

"Whoa," Lieutenant Brooks growled at his remount, yanking on the bit. "Now what," he muttered under his breath, wheeling his horse around and galloping back to the first wagon. Sergeant O'Malley reined around to look after the lieutenant.

Cam seized the moment. "Sorry, Patch," he said, sharply jerking his bay directly in front of Patch's horse and heading for the scrub oak on the far side of the road. As he shot past Patch's pony, he grabbed the bridle, yanking the horse's head to the side, sending the startled animal to the ground and Patch rolling across the road.

A shout from behind was followed instantly by the boom of Sharps. A powerful blow struck Cam in the shoulder, knocking him from the saddle. He bounced off a twisted oak and slammed to the ground. He leaped to his feet and blindly stumbled through the thick undergrowth, oblivious as to direction, hoping only to manage his escape.

Behind, came the crash of pursuit.

He paused. His head swam, and he grabbed a stunted oak for support. He had to find refuge and fast before he passed out. He stumbled forward, striking a shallow wash free of underbrush. He followed it to a narrow creek meandering down the rock-strewn hill. He hesitated. His only stroke of good luck was that the creek bed was rocky. Staying out of the water, he stumbled upstream along the bed until he spotted a second wash opening into the creek.

Hastily, he staggered up the wash until he found a tangle of winter-dead vines and berry briars over a long-fallen oak. Ignoring the pain throbbing in his shoulder, he dropped to his knees and wormed his way under the briars, closing his eyes as he felt the tiny thorns tearing at his face. Once inside, he curled into a ball. He strained his ears for the sound of pursuit, but within seconds, he slipped into unconsciousness.

Half-an-hour later, Lieutenant Brooks barked at O'Malley. "We've searched long enough for the thief, Sergeant. Call Private Melder in, and let's get the ladies on into Limestone."

"At least we know he's wounded, Lieutenant. Must have been a pint of blood on the saddle. Probably, he's crawled in some hole to die like the mongrel he is."

Milly gasped and pressed her hand to her lips when she heard the sergeant. Her eyes scanned the thick scrub oak into which Cam had disappeared. At her side, Ellie whispered. "Is Cam dead, Milly?"

The young woman forced a smile. "No. He isn't dead." She hoped in her heart she was right.

"What's he going to do out here all by himself?"

Milly shook her head. She had no answer for her sister.

As the wagons lurched forward, and before Private Melder had taken up his position as drag, Blue Stick silently dropped off the rear of the wagon and, like a ghost, vanished into the tangle of scrub oak.

Chapter Sixteen

The curtain of darkness enveloping Cam slowly faded as he struggled back into a fuzzy awareness of time and place. He shivered against the cold, and as the drug of unconsciousness wore off, he became aware of the searing pain in his shoulder. He closed his eyes and clenched his teeth against the shards of fire radiating from his shoulder.

Suddenly, the briars shook as a pole penetrated the thick patch of thorns. Cam froze, then relaxed, as a voice cracked with age said. "Soldiers go."

He peered up through the briars, spotting an outline broken by the briars. "Blue Stick?"

"Come. Soldiers go."

Moving slowly so as not to jar his arm, Cam eased from under the briars. His sleeve was soaked with blood. He tried to stand, but a wave of dizziness swept over him. Blue Stick hooked a bony arm around Cam's waist. Exhibiting surprising strength for such a bent and withered body, he pulled Cam to his feet. "Come."

Cam didn't protest. His head spun, but he continued stumbling through the scrub oak whilst leaning on the old Comanche. He lost track of time.

Once or twice, Blue Stick paused to orient himself. Each time, he gave a brief nod, then altered his direction accordingly. As unerring as a bee to honey, Blue Stick half-led, half-carried, Cam through the scrub, over several dry washes, and finally around a rocky hill into a cave, the mouth of which was hidden behind decades-old oak and cedar. Inside, Blue Stick lowered Cam to the rocky floor and leaned him up against a wall. "Make fire."

As the fire came to life, Blue Stick rummaged through a beaded bag. Retiring deeper into the cave, he returned with a gourd of water and a hide bowl. He placed a few rocks in the fire, then filled the bowl with water. "Eat," he said, handing Cam a petal of peyote and the gourd of water to wash it down.

Still drifting in and out of consciousness, Cam had neither the energy nor inclination to argue. The pain in his shoulder had spread to every nerve in his body. Woodenly, he did as the old man said.

Soon, the rocks were hot, and using two green branches to fish them from the fire, Blue Stick dropped the rocks into the bowl of water. After cleansing the wound with hot water, he packed it with a mixture of roots from his bag, then wrapped the shoulder. He sat back on his heels and, satisfied with his handiwork, nodded. "Now, we eat."

As the wagon train drew near to Limestone, Victor Keith elbowed Ira and said, "You can come over to my house and ride my pony anytime you want, Ira."

Ira looked around at his friend. "You don't have a pony."

Victor shrugged. "Not yet, but Ma says she'll talk to Pa. Won't that be swell?"

"Sure will." Ira shook his head. "My Pa was going to buy me a horse once."

"What happened to your Pa?"

Ira's face grew solemn. "He's dead."

The young boy grimaced. "Gosh. I'd sure hate for my Pa to die. I'm sorry about yours."

"That's all right. It was back in San Antonio. That's why we come up here. So Milly could teach."

Victor frowned. "Couldn't she teach back there?"

Suddenly, Ira realized he had said too much. "No."

"Why not?"

"She just couldn't." Ira stared off toward Limestone.

Victor pursued the matter. "But, why not? Wasn't she smart enough?"

Angrily, Ira turned on Victor. "She's smarter than anyone you'll ever know."

With mischievousness gleaming in his eyes, Victor innocently asked, "Then why couldn't she teach in San Antonio?"

Ira glared at his friend. "I told you. She just couldn't."

Delighted that Ira was irritated, Victor teased him some more. "That's no reason. I bet that's what it was. She wasn't smart enough to be a teacher."

By now, Ira was furious. "You say that again, and I'll punch you in the nose. You hear?"

Victor leaned back, sobered by his friend's reaction. "Gosh, Ira. I didn't mean to make you mad. I was just teasing you. You don't have to tell me if you don't want to."

Ira cooled off quickly. He considered what he should do. "Look. We're good friends, aren't we?"

"Sure we are."

"If I tell you something, will you promise never, never to tell anyone? Swear on a stack of Bibles?"

Lured by the sudden display of intrigue, Victor nodded. "I promise."

"Cross your heart."

Victor crossed it.

"Okay. And remember, you promised not to tell anyone, ever."

Sheriff John Potter studied the cave in which the wagon train had camped and then the sign leading to the clearing where the horses had been corralled. On the way back to the cave, he spotted tracks leading up the ridge.

Potter had tracked enough rustlers, rogue Indians, stolen cattle, and two-bit outlaws that he easily put together the silent story left behind by the tracks. And when he discovered the numerous shoed hoof prints over the imprints left by the wagon wheels, he knew several riders had been in the cave since the train had pulled out.

"Now, why would they come back?" He muttered to his horse as he swung into the saddle and stared down at the sign. With a click of his tongue, he turned his pony on their trail as he left the cave, but as soon as the tracks hit the road, the group split, two heading to Limestone, one south through the scrub, and one back west, toward Menard.

Three miles down the road, Sheriff Potter reined up as a buzzard, startled by his approach, burst from the underbrush along the side of the road. He ignored the buzzard, figuring it had been feasting upon the usual carrion left behind by wolves or mountain lions. He touched his heels to his pony's flanks.

Suddenly, a tiny flash of sunlight in the underbrush from which the buzzard had flown arrested his attention. He reined up. Curious, he rode over to the object. "What's this?" he muttered, spotting the muzzle of a revolver protruding from under a tangle of briars.

Dismounting, he reached for the muzzle, then froze. "Dear Lord," he whispered, staring into the underbrush at the near naked bodies of Blackjack and Sundown.

He could do nothing for the two. He searched through the clothes that had been sliced from their dead bodies. Nothing to identify them. He spread the ripped clothes over the bodies as best he could, hoping to deter the buzzards from their grisly task, at least until he could return with a wagon.

He swung into the saddle and kicked his pony

into a gallop. He wanted to get the bodies back to town while there were still enough features to establish an identity.

To his disappointment, when the bodies were brought back in, they were beyond identification.

A celebration greeted the small wagon train when it pulled into Limestone. The husbands were there to meet their families, and Mayor Peter Watts and Reverend Marcus Reeves, along with Miss Abigail Webster, head of the local Women's Bible Study, were on-hand to welcome their new schoolmarm.

Penelope Keith looked on in anguish as Lieutenant Brooks shackled Patch to a post inside the livery until morning. Patch smiled sadly at her.

From where he sat, he saw her go up to her father. She spoke to him, and he looked at Patch, then shook his head and gestured for Penelope to climb into the wagon. For a moment, she refused to budge. Her father gestured to the wagon once again. She looked around at Patch. Even from this distance, he saw the determination in her eyes. To his surprise and dismay, however, she climbed into the wagon.

Once on the seat, she looked back and nodded. A faint smile played over her lips.

Chapter Seventeen

That night, in their small, neat cabin, the three Barretts sat around a small table, heads bowed and holding hands while Milly murmured a heartfelt prayer over their meal of salted pork and fried potatoes.

Ira looked up when she finished, his eyes filled with awe. "Is this house really ours, Milly? Huh? Is it?"

She smiled at him and patted Ellie's hand. "It's the house for the teacher. It's ours now, as long as we want to stay."

The young boy looked around the two-room cabin. "It's nice. Not as nice as the one we had in San Antonio, but a heap fancier than New Braunfels."

Milly scolded him. "What did I tell you about San Antonio? You can't tell anyone we came from there. You remember? You don't ever mention the word."

Guilt flooded through the boy as he thought of having revealed the secret to Victor. But, he reminded himself, Victor would never repeat the secret. He had promised. He had even crossed his heart.

Harshly, she questioned him. "You haven't said anything, have you?"

To cover the embarrassment coloring his cheeks, he responded with a feigned sense of outrage at her doubting him. "I told you I wouldn't, didn't I?" The reply wasn't exactly a lie.

Her face softened. "I'm sorry, Ira. It's just that it is so important to all of us."

His cheeks burned with shame. "I know, sis."

Ira tossed and turned that night, trying to convince himself that Victor would indeed remain silent.

After Milly tucked the two children into bed, she rolled some salt pork and biscuits in oilcloth and slipped into her coat to ward off the chill. Guilt at keeping quiet about the identity of the robbers continued to eat at her.

She had decided the only way to assuage her conscience was to tell Patch all she knew and make him promise not to reveal how he learned it.

Private Melder checked her small bundle. "He's over there. In the corner."

Warily, Patch studied her. "I'm surprised to see you."

She hesitated. "Why? Because of the robbery?"

"Something like that."

With a soft laugh, she handed him the small bundle of food. "I don't believe you were part of it. Now, here. Eat. It isn't much, but it'll fill you up."

A broad grin played over his face. "My belly's

been gnawing at my backbone," he said, tearing off a chunk of salt pork.

Milly glanced over her shoulder, then lowered her voice. "I know something about the robbers, but you have to promise you won't tell anyone where you heard it."

In the darkness, his facial features were difficult to discern, but she could make out the frown on his forehead. After a moment, he replied. "I won't."

She glanced around at the young private once again. He was sitting in the lantern light playing a game of solitaire. She turned back around and told Patch about seeing the two men from the window. "One of them was the one who robbed us. The other man was Hez Clutter. You remember him from the wagon train?"

Patch nodded. "I remember."

"He's one of Brock's, so he might be involved. I don't know for sure, but I did see Hez talking to the man who robbed us. But remember, you can't tell anyone I told you."

For a few moments, Patch remained silent. "I won't, but why not? Can't you tell me?"

She shook her head. "My life could be ruined."

Even in the shadows, she saw a small, a sad smile play over his lips. "I hope not, Miss Milly. I sure do hope not."

When Cam awakened, Blue Stick was nowhere to be seen. He lay without moving, not wanting to jar his shoulder. Tentatively, he touched his fingers to the bandage. There was no pain. He pressed harder and winced as a sliver of pain shot out from the wound. He quickly removed his hand. Slowly, the pain eased, only to be replaced by a nagging itch on one side of his face. He rubbed at it.

At that moment, Blue Stick returned. He halted when he saw Cam was awake. With a brief nod, he knelt by the fire and dipped the gourd into the hide bowl. He offered it to Cam. "Sit. Drink."

Reluctantly, Cam struggled to sit up, clenching his teeth against the anticipated pain. It came, but not in the severe waves he expected.

Blue Stick saw the surprise on Cam's face. He pointed to the shoulder. "Not bad. Bullet go through. Nice hole." He picked up another bowl and showed it to Cam. "Poultice. Make well." He offered Cam the gourd again. "Drink. Good."

"Thanks." Cam nodded and took the gourd. He wrinkled his nose at the smell.

Blue Stick grinned. "Drink."

Taking a deep breath, Cam turned the gourd up and downed the rank-smelling mixture as quickly as possible. He grimaced. The concoction tasted worse than it smelled, and it smelled worse than a sheepherder's socks. Somehow, he managed to get it down and keep it down.

He shivered and handed the gourd to Blue Stick whose grin grew wider. "Sleep now," said the old Indian. "Better in the morning."

"I hope so," Cam replied, scratching at the itch on the side of his face.

Brock and Hatfield camped outside of Limestone, preferring to ride in during daylight. Night drifters drew too much attention.

Early in the morning, while Hatfield slept soundly, Brock crept from his blankets and slipped a knife between Hatfield's ribs and into his heart. With a grunt of satisfaction, he wiped the knife on his greasy trousers and jammed Hatfield's share of the loot into his own pocket.

He dragged the dead man to a nearby gully and rolled him over the side, then returned to the fire and crawled back under his own blankets.

He slept like a baby.

The temperature dropped during the night and next morning, when Milly looked out the window of their new home, she caught her breath at the beauty of the sunlight glittering on the frost covering the ground. Just like a picture, she thought, planning to wake the children so they could see.

Abruptly, she froze, then jerked back from the window. Her heart thudded against her chest. "It can't be," she mumbled in shock. She leaned forward, peering around the corner of the window at the lone cowpoke riding down the street.

Joe Brock! She was certain it was Brock. She hadn't seen him since the wagon train reached Menard, but she could never forget the cold eyes and rocky features of the bearded man. What was he doing here in Limestone? Did he know her secret? He must, for the robber knew, and now she was convinced the robber worked for Brock.

Fortunately, the day was Saturday. No school, which meant they could stay in the house without arousing suspicion. Even as she peered from the window, she saw the cavalry patrol ride out with

Patch in the middle. She hoped the information she had passed along to him would help.

When Cam awakened, he felt refreshed. His face still itched, and his arm was still sore, but whatever the poultice was that Blue Stick had used, it had worked miracles. Two rabbits broiled over the fire. His stomach growled. He patted it. "Smells good," he said, nodding to Blue Stick. "Hungry." He rubbed his belly.

The old Indian stared at him impassively, then dipped the gourd in the hide bowl and offered it to Cam. "Drink. Make well."

"Oh, no," Cam muttered, seeing the same dark mixture that had gagged him earlier. He shook his head.

Blue Stick held the gourd to him. "Drink, then eat."

Cam shook his head and pointed to the rabbit. "Eat, then drink."

"No." Blue Stick shook his head. "Eat, drink, get sick. Drink, eat, not get sick."

Rolling his eyes, Cam knew he had no choice. Whatever Blue Stick had been pouring down him worked. He stared at the smaller man who kept the gourd in his outstretched hand. Reluctantly, Cam took it. "Eat. Get sick? Drink, eat, not get sick?"

Blue Stick nodded. Cam drew a deep breath. "Watch out stomach, here it comes." Half-a-dozen large gulps did the job. Cam lowered the empty gourd and shivered.

The old Indian's eyes laughed. He tore off a leg

of rabbit and handed it to Cam who ravenously bit into the tender, white meat.

As they ate, Cam indicated his shoulder. "How long before I can be on horse?"

"Two–three suns," Blue Stick replied, pulling a strip of rabbit from the bone and poking it between his thin lips. He glanced into the darkness behind them, deeper into the cave. "Me find two horses, guns. Good horses, guns."

Cam didn't ask any questions about where Blue Stick found the guns and horses. "Good," he said, washing the last of the rabbit down with several large swallows of water. As anxious as he was to find the real robbers, he knew that right now there was no way he could fork a saddle.

A great weariness settled over him. A combination of the concoction Blue Stick poured down him and a full stomach made him sleepy. He lay back and stared at the dancing shadows cast by the fire on the ceiling of the cave.

He wondered about Patch. He guessed that, by now, Patch was locked up in the Menard jail. His bone-weary mind tried to decide just what he should do next, but the desire for sleep was over-powering.

Absently, he scratched the side of his face. Suddenly, he paused, then lightly touched the side of his face. Tiny blisters covered his skin.

He frowned, puzzled, then abruptly, he slammed his eyes closed and cursed. He touched the blisters again, and again broke into a string of curses. "That just about puts icing on the cake," he growled. "Poison ivy."

Chapter Eighteen

When the patrol reached Menard, Patch was re-manded to the custody of the sheriff, who promptly locked him in a single cell. Afterward, Lieutenant Brooks laid out the evidence, adding, "Those two did go after the boy, Sheriff. The boy verified that part of the story. Personally, I figure they did it to throw the blame off them."

The lieutenant's theory had holes in it big enough to run a herd of Mexican steers through, but Potter kept quiet, thanking the lieutenant instead. After Brooks left, the sheriff plopped down behind his desk. He pulled out a bag of Bull Durham. He saw Patch eying it. "Smoke?"

"I'd appreciate one."

Potter poured out his makings, used his teeth to tighten the string, then tossed it through the bars to Patch. He rolled his cigarette. "Now, you want to tell me what happened?"

Uncertain as to whether the sheriff and Brock had

any connection, Patch decided to keep Milly's disclosure from the night before to himself, at least for the time being. Instead, he related the events of the previous day, pausing to return the bag of Bull Durham.

Sheriff Potter listened carefully, fitting pieces of the young man's story into the story he had read in the sign. "How long before you found the boy?"

"Not long. Thirty minutes more or less. A small valley. He was standing there all by hisself."

"So, you and Cam was gone for about an hour?"

"Yep."

"What then?"

Patch shrugged. "When we got back, the army boys was there. The ladies were all shouting that me and Cam had told them owlhoots where to find the payroll."

Potter pursed his lips, nodded, then casually asked. "Why did Cam run if he was innocent?"

For a moment, Patch hesitated, remembering Cam's concern with the army asking questions. "I don't know, Sheriff. I truly don't know why he did it. First thing I knew, he made a break and grabbed my horse by the bridle, tossing me to the ground."

The sheriff arched an eyebrow. "Why would he do that, do you think?"

Patch knew without a doubt. Cam didn't want to involve him. "Truth is sheriff, I'd've helped Cam escape, but he didn't want me involved."

"So, he pulled your horse down so you couldn't help." Sheriff Potter eyed Patch shrewdly. "That's what you're telling me?"

Looking the sheriff square in the eyes, Patch nodded. "Yes, sir. That's exactly what I'm telling you."

For several moments, the sheriff studied him. There were a couple weak spots in the young man's story, but for the most part, Sheriff Potter figured Patch had told him the truth.

The young cowpoke gripped the bars. "Sheriff. You believe me?"

"Makes no difference what I believe, son. It's what the judge and jury believe."

Patch gulped, his Adam's apple bobbing up and down. "Sheriff. This ain't a vigilante town, is it?"

Potter felt sorry for the young man. "Don't worry none about that. Last time a jasper tried to take the law in his own hands, we buried him next day." He nodded to the bunk. "Just take it easy. Ain't nothing you can do nohow."

Patch remained standing, clutching the bars, Milly's story burning a hole in his brain just like a red-hot coal burns a hole in a jasper's jeans. Maybe he should tell the sheriff, but what if the sheriff and Brock were in cahoots? Maybe later, he told himself. Find out the lay of the land first.

The sheriff believed Patch's story. They were gone from the camp an hour. Victor Keith verified that part, at least according to the lieutenant. *Yes, sir*, Potter thought. They were gone just long enough for someone to set them up good to take the blame. The one part of the incident that told him Cam was innocent was the question of how Victor Keith ended up a mile or so away. Who carried him out there? It couldn't have been Cam or Patch. They were back in camp.

He stroked his mustache, puzzling over the enigma. Now who could have planned such a slick robbery? It had to be someone who knew where the payroll was hidden. He knew he hadn't, and he believed strongly that Cam and Patch had no hand in it. That left Asplund or Higgins. But why? What could they gain robbing from their own company? Suspicions were one thing, but they had to be saddled with some kind of reason, some motives.

The sheriff ambled onto the porch and plopped down on the rope seat of his straight back chair next to the slab door. Idly, he studied the street as he tried fitting various pieces into the puzzle. Why were Cam and Patch singled out? Why someone like Cam, a newcomer? That's what puzzled him. Did Asplund or Higgins know something about the man? Was it connected with his trips to Mason? Could that have been the reason he ran? Or was he indeed part of the robbery? He muttered a curse.

Sunday morning, Milly rose early. Anxiously, she peered from the window, wondering where Brock had spent the night. She knew she and the children had to attend Sunday services. That the school-teacher attend church regularly had been made clear before the town hired her.

She prayed silently that he would not spot her and the children as they made their way to church. Maybe Brock was sleeping off drunkness from the night before.

* * *

During the service, the Reverend Reeves introduced her and her brother and sister to the congregation. After the service, benches were moved aside and tables set up in the sanctuary. Covered baskets laden with meats, side dishes, and bread were spread, and the entire congregation enjoyed a community dinner honoring their new teacher.

Milly beamed at Ira and Ellie. Finally, they had found a home. She glanced out the window at the bright sunlight spilling over the rugged hills. Now, if only Brock would leave town.

The next morning, to Milly's delight, less than an hour before she would ring the bell for school, Brock rode out of Limestone. Her spirits soared.

Later, Brock pulled up on the rim of a rocky ledge overlooking the road to Menard. Hurriedly, he backed his horse, then dismounted and crept back to the rim.

Below, Sheriff Potter rode toward Menard. Brock frowned and scratched his wiry beard with thick fingers. He wasn't anxious to cross paths with the sheriff out here. So soon after the robbery, Potter would have a thousand questions.

Building a small fire, he decided to wait a spell.

Later that same morning, his arm in a sling and the side of his face covered with a pasty concoction that smelled worse than the brew the old Comanche had made him drink, Cam and Blue Stick rode from the cave with the old man leading the way. Cam looked over the rugged country about him. "We heading north?"

Without looking back, Blue Stick nodded.

"Is that where Menard is?"

"Menard that way," he replied, pointing south-west.

"That where I want to go. To Menard."

Blue Stick reined up and looked at Cam with impassive eyes. "Big trouble."

"Maybe, but that's the only place I know to start looking for whoever robbed the payroll. Besides, I need to find out about Patch," he added.

"Sheriff look for you."

With a sigh of frustration, Cam said. "I know. That's one reason I wish I didn't have to go back to Menard, but whoever did it had to come from there. That was the only place they could have learned about the payroll."

The old Indian gestured north. "Smart we go to Indian country. Soldiers not look there."

Cam stubbornly shook his head. "Menard."

With stoic compliance, Blue Stick reined his pony around and led the way through the scrub oak and briar tangles.

At any moment, Cam kept expecting to intersect the road to Menard, but all day, Blue Stick twisted and turned through the chaparral. Just before dark, they pulled up under a rocky ledge. "Camp here," the old Indian announced.

Cam didn't argue. His shoulder was sore, but the jarring ride had not opened the wound.

"Sure could use a cup of coffee," Cam muttered, tearing off a piece of jerky and washing it down with water. Blue Stick grunted. Beyond the firelight, night fell over the countryside.

Suddenly, a voice called from the darkness. "Hello, anyone there?"

Cam shucked his six-gun. "Come on in, friend, but come easy."

"Don't fret none on me, partner," the voice called back. Moments later, a rider appeared.

"Well, I'll be," Cam muttered, holstering his six-gun. "Joe Brock. Surprised to see you out here."

Brock gaped, shocked to see Cam. He figured the deputy was in jail. Quickly, he covered his surprise. "Howdy there, Deputy." He cut his black eyes toward Blue Stick and frowned. "Didn't expect to see you out here with a Redskin."

"His name's Blue Stick," Cam said, offering no explanation for the old man's being there.

Brock frowned at the plaster on Cam's face and the sling around his neck. "What happened to you? Looks like you been rode hard and put away wet."

Cam's ears burned. "Poison ivy." Changing the subject, he glanced at Brock's saddlebags. "Hope you got makings for coffee with you."

With a grin, Brock dismounted. "You got water, I got the makings."

Within minutes, coffee was boiling, and the rich flavor assailed Cam's nostrils. "Smells mighty good," he muttered. He glanced at Brock. "How was the prospecting? You weren't in Limestone long."

The big man shook his head, curiosity eating at his patience. "Too much like work. What about you? I heard from one of the miners something about a payroll being took." He studied Cam narrowly, looking for any sign of duplicity.

With casual aplomb, Cam grunted. "Reckon you heard right."

"Any idea who pulled it off?" Brock tossed Cam a cup and reached for the coffee pot.

Holding out the cup as Brock poured, Cam replied succinctly, "Nope."

Unable to suppress his overwhelming curiosity, Brock asked. "What about Patch? He stay in Limestone?"

With a grin, Cam grunted. "Yep. I think he was a little sweet on the Keith girl."

Brock chuckled despite his growing confusion. Both Cam and Patch should have been arrested. What could have gone wrong? "Quite a looker, as I remember." He sipped his coffee and leaned back on one elbow. Feigning a yawn, he asked, "Why ain't you with the sheriff?"

Cam frowned. "What do you mean? The sheriff's in Menard."

Arching an eyebrow, Brock shook his head. "Don't think so, Deputy. I passed him this morning, and he was heading for Limestone."

"Limestone?"

"Yep." Brock sipped his coffee, hoping Cam would believe his lie. "I'd figured you would have passed him on the road."

Cam's pulse sped up. Sheriff Potter being out of town was one less worry—one less big worry. He drained his coffee and poured the grounds on the fire. He tossed the cup to Brock and pushed to his feet. "Well, reckon as how the sheriff's out of town,

I best be riding in." He glanced at Blue Stick. "It don't do for a town to be without the law."

Blue Stick nodded gravely and rose to his feet.

As they rode into the darkness, Joe Brock sneered. "Ride on in, Deputy. Sheriff Potter will give you a reception you ain't likely to forget."

Chapter Nineteen

Bathed in starlight, the small town slept peacefully. Cam and Blue Stick reined up in a small copse of scrub oak. "I'll go in," he whispered, handing the old man the reins and dismounting. "You wait."

Staying in the shadows, Cam ghosted into town, finally crouching in the shadows along the side of the jail. He peered through a window into the dimly lit room. Except for Patch, it was empty.

Brock had been right. Potter was nowhere around.

Moving silently, Cam crept to the rear of the jail to the cell window. He tossed a pebble inside, then another. "Patch," he whispered. "Patch."

"Cam? That you?"

"Quiet. I'm going to break you out of here while the sheriff's gone."

"Huh? The sheriff ain't gone."

Cam's blood ran cold. "What?"

"The sheriff is here in town. Hurry up. I know who pulled off the robbery."

Cam searched the darkness about him. "Who?"

"Milly Barrett told me. Remember Hez Clutter? He was one of Brock's men. He was the youngest. Milly told me she saw him talking to the hombre what took the payroll."

"Did you tell the sheriff?"

"Not yet. I don't know if he's in with them or not."

Squinting into the night for any movement, Cam replied. "I can't believe he is. He's a good man. Fair too. Was Brock part of it?"

"She didn't know. All she knew was she saw Clutter talking to this other feller. Now hurry up. Clutter is down in Cherry Springs. Get me out and let's run him down. The sheriff will have to believe us then."

A cold voice froze both men. "Maybe he does now."

Cam jerked around. A dark silhouette stood facing him at the corner of the jail. A familiar voice spoke. "Glad you came back, Cam. It'll make things easier. Let's just go inside and talk it all over."

There was nothing Cam wanted to do more, but La Grange was still hanging over his head. "Sorry, Sheriff. I can't. I got work to do."

"Don't make a mistake, boy. Let the law take care of it."

Cam believed the sheriff, but he didn't believe the law. "Sheriff, Patch had nothing to do with anything. Somebody deliberately put the blame on us."

"I know you caught the blame. Now, come on in.

You know I can't let you ride out of town." The sharp click of a hammer being cocked added an exclamation mark to his declaration.

The words took Cam by surprise.

From the window, Patch whispered. "Did you hear that, Cam? Did you hear that?"

"I heard, but there's more."

The sheriff's deep voice rolled through the darkness. "You mean La Grange?"

Instantly, Cam grew wary. "I don't know what you're talking about. I never been to La—"

At that moment, a dull thud interrupted Cam, and Sheriff Potter groaned and crumpled to the ground. Blue Stick's thin voice cut through the night. "We go."

"We'll be back," the lanky cowpoke whispered to Patch as he followed Blue Stick's fleeting shadow down the alley.

Low over their horses's necks, Cam and Blue Stick raced over the road leading back to the camp where they had left Joe Brock.

The big man had some questions to answer. First, about Sheriff Potter's sudden appearance in Menard when he was supposed to be in Limestone, and second, about Hez Clutter.

As Cam had half-expected, the camp was long deserted, which convinced him that Brock had deliberately lied about the sheriff being in Limestone. And the only reason he would lie was because he had a hand in the robbery somehow.

Cam sat in his saddle studying the ashes of the campfire, wishing he had his hands on Joe Brock.

However, he didn't want to waste time tracking Brock when he knew where Clutter was.

The two continued toward Mason, where they took the road southeast to Cherry Springs. Cam remembered Fort McKavett and the trail hands who had come in with the wagon train. He thought he could probably recognize the young man, although he wasn't positive.

The morning dawned bright and clear in Limestone. Milly hummed as she made breakfast. The first two days of school had gone well. She shook her head at just how fine their lives were turning out.

Just as she turned to awaken Ira and Ellie, she spotted a small buggy turn the corner and head in her direction. Mayor Peter Watts was driving, and at his side sat Reverend Marcus Reeves. Behind them, Miss Abigail Webster, head of the local Women's Bible Study, and Lydia Morrison were perched primly on the edge of their seats, their wrinkled faces pinched into sour frowns. Three men on horses trotted behind.

The buggy stopped in front. The men jumped down, then helped the women step from the buggy. Their countenances were grim as they marched to the door. The three riders remained in their saddles.

Milly frowned, puzzled. And then, with a sudden sickening nausea churning her stomach, she knew why they were here. The sharp knock at the door startled her. She drew her tongue over her dry lips and struggled to compose herself. With as much dignity as she could muster, she opened the door.

Forcing a smile, she greeted them. "Why Mayor Watts, Reverend Reeves. This is a surprise."

Lydia Morrison spoke up. "It shouldn't be. You know why we're here."

As sweetly as she could, Milly replied. "I'm sorry, but I don't. Would you like to come in? It's chilly outside."

The reverend started in, but the mayor stopped him and cleared his throat before speaking. "This is a very delicate matter, Miss Barrett. Very delicate."

Abigail Webster pinched her lips together like she was holding a straight pin. "Do your job, Peter. We have the sanctity of our town to think of."

Mayor Watts coughed into his fist. He glanced at the reverend, who nodded for the mayor to continue. "Miss Barrett. It has come to our attention—I mean, a rumor came to our attention that—" he hesitated, "that—ah—"

Lydia Morrison interrupted, her strident voice braying with hate. "Are you and your brother and sister Injun half-breeds?"

Milly stared at her in shock. Behind her, she heard a gasp and turned to see Ellie disappear into the bedroom.

Reverend Reeves cleared his throat. "I don't know how this could be true, Miss Barrett," he said. "Your blond hair, your fair complexion. We—I mean, I—" he ducked his head.

Her ears pounded with the rush of blood.

Before she could respond, Abigail Webster sniffed. "It seems the story came from your brother, who told Victor Keith that you were a half-breed, and that's why you couldn't teach in San Antonio."

Milly clenched her fists, fighting the tears blinding her vision. She blinked her eyes, spilling the tears down her cheeks. She tried unsuccessfully to swallow the burning lump in her throat. She wanted to strike out, to hurt someone as much as she hurt, but she held her composure.

Mayor Watts coughed. "Is the story true, Miss Barrett?"

Setting her jaw, she looked him directly in the eye. "Yes," she replied in a soft, firm voice with as much dignity as she could muster.

The two women gasped. Lydia Morrison declared. "I knew something was wrong when she took that savage into her wagon, but I never figured this."

The mayor continued, his voice hard and cold now that he had learned the truth. "I'm afraid the town can no longer offer you a teaching position, Miss Barr—" He caught himself before he addressed a half-breed with an appellation of courtesy. "We cannot offer you the teaching position. Consequently, you and your brother and sister must find other accommodations."

"Not in Limestone," Abigail Webster screeched. "Not in Limestone."

"As a gesture of our goodwill," announced Reverend Reeves pompously, "we will assist you in loading your belongings." The three men dismounted and approached the open door, while a fourth pulled up in front of the house with her wagon and team.

As Milly tearfully watched the men load her meager belongings into the wagon, she promised herself she would never again try to hide the truth. She was what she was. Her brother and sister were what they were.

Maybe she had been wrong to hide the truth.

No longer.

Chapter Twenty

Cam rode into the small village of Cherry Springs in mid-afternoon, having left Blue Stick on a rocky ridge covered with scrub cedar overlooking the small town. The old Indian had protested, but Cam insisted. Blue Stick was thin as a leather strap when they first met, and it appeared to Cam the old man had become even thinner. He needed rest.

Hez Clutter was not hard to find. No drunk with money to burn is. In the first saloon, Cam heard a couple cowpokes laughing about the wild and drunken shebang Clutter had thrown the night before.

"I reckon he sure done give the girls at Miss Dora's a good time, you suppose?"

The other cowpoke guffawed. "Sure wouldn't surprise me none at all."

An hour later, a bleary-eyed cowpoke stumbled through the batwing doors and was greeted with hoorahs and whoopees. Instantly, Cam recognized the young man. Hez Clutter.

Cam glanced in the mirror behind the bar. He started momentarily, failing to recognize the stranger staring back at him. The last few days had ridden him hard. His face was covered with scabbed-over scratches from the briars as well as remnants of the poultice Blue Stick had daubed on his face for poison ivy, along with a week's worth of whiskers and a dozen pounds of grime. He didn't reckon he looked much like he did a week earlier.

The young man lost no time in starting the party, ordering drinks for the house even before he reached the bar.

Cam took a table in the rear of the saloon, nursing a mug of warm beer, puzzling over just how he was going to get Clutter alone.

His chance came just before midnight when the young man drunkenly declared he was heading for Miss Dora's.

"I reckon I'll just go along with you," one of the revelers laughed.

"Not with me," Clutter declared. "I don't need no help." He slapped another greenback on the bar. "Drinks for the house, bartender."

Cam chose that moment to slip out the rear and station himself in the shadows between the saloon and Miss Dora's next door.

When young Hez Clutter staggered by, Cam cold-cocked him.

Ten minutes later, on the ridge overlooking

Cherry Springs, Cam dumped Clutter on the ground at Blue Stick's feet.

When Clutter awoke next morning, he lay spread-eagled on the ground, his arms and legs tightly bound. "Hey! What's going in?" He jerked on the ropes.

Cam looked up from the small fire. "Not much, boy. I just wanted a chance to have a little talk with you. A few questions, then I'll put you on your way."

"I ain't answering no questions. Not to you or no one." He tried to sound belligerent but failed miserably.

With a faint grin, Cam rose and stared down at Clutter. "Oh, I reckon you will. We got ways. Indian ways."

The young man cut his eyes fearfully toward Blue Stick. They grew wider when the old Indian pulled out a wicked looking knife from the beaded sheath on his slender hip. He swallowed hard.

Cam drawled. "You appear a little inclined not to cooperate, boy. Well, I'll tell you how Comanches encourage folks like you to talk. They lop off one of your fingers and roast it over the fire. Then they got the bad habit of eating it in front you."

Sweat beaded Clutter's face. "You're a white man. You wouldn't let him do that to another white man."

Cam leered at the frightened young man. "Don't you go counting on that. Now, all I want to know is who was behind stealing the money from the wagon train."

Clutter's eyes widened in recognition. "I remember you. That deputy. Cameron."

"I wouldn't worry about me, boy. You best worry about you."

"I don't know anything about a payroll."

Cam chuckled. "I didn't say anything about a payroll. If you didn't have a hand in it, how did you know it was a payroll?" He shook his head and motioned to Blue Stick. "Show this hardhead we mean business, old man."

Clutter's eyes grew wide as Blue Stick knelt, placing his knee on Clutter's wrist to still his hand. The old man grabbed a finger.

The young man moaned. His chest heaved as he sucked in great breaths of air. He blubbered. "Brock. Joe Brock. He planned it. He figured you was running from the bank robbery in La Grange, and you'd be an easy jasper to put the blame on. Honest."

"Brock, huh? How much was your share?"

Tears rolling down his cheeks, he stammered. "Two hundred and fifty."

Cam rolled his eyes. "Two fifty out of ten thousand. You're dumber than I thought."

Clutter gaped in surprise. "Ten thousand? There wasn't no ten thousand in them bags. It was two thousand."

It was Cam's turn to gape. "Two?" He hesitated. "If there was only two, Brock snookered you."

"Honest, Cameron. It was only two. I saw Brock take it out of the saddlebags."

Cam studied the struggling cowpoke. "He could

have just told you that. Did you look in the saddle-bags?"

"No, but Brock was mad, killing mad. He killed Blackjack and Sundown right then. Two thousand was all there was." He struggled against his bonds. "Please. That's the truth."

Cam shook his head and pursed his lips. He stared without seeing at the spread-eagled cowpoke. Another unexpected twist had been added to the already convoluted incident. "All right, Blue Stick. Let him go."

The old Indian looked around, a gleam in his dark eyes and a crooked grin on his face. "Me only take one finger. Then turn loose."

Hez Clutter bawled like a baby.

Cam knelt at the young man's side and fished through his pockets. He pulled out a handful of wadded bills. "You're going back to Menard. Sheriff Potter will be glad to see you," he said, slipping the bills into his saddlebags.

They camped halfway between Cherry Springs and Mason that night. Cam couldn't help noticing Blue Stick ate very little. The old man's breathing had grown labored.

Upon arising next morning, Cam was surprised to see the old Indian still sleeping, unlike the previous mornings when he was squatting at the fire, poking at the coals and broiling meat on spits.

Throughout the day, Cam watched the old Indian from the corner of his eye. A few miles west of Mason, they pulled up at the San Saba River to fill their canteens and rest their ponies.

The temperature was rising, the cold front having drifted on south and replaced with southwesterly breezes off the Gulf of Mexico. If the weather followed its course, there would be rain by dark.

Hez Clutter was climbing back in his saddle when the rifle boomed. As if a great hand had jerked him backward, the young man flew out of his saddle over the haunches of his horse.

Cam shucked his six-gun and dropped behind a rock. A hundred yards beyond the river, a cloud of white smoke drifted up from behind a limestone boulder. Moments later, the sound of hoof beats echoed over the rocky ground.

Muttering a curse, Cam scrabbled through the underbrush and boulders to the young cowpoke. Clutter's breath came in raw gasps, and bright red blood bubbled from his chest with each gasp. Pain glazed his eyes. He forced a grin. "Looks like the sheriff's going to be disappointed, don't it?" He tried to laugh, but a series of racking coughs shook his body. And then he died.

Cam stared at the dead man for a few seconds, then muttered a curse. He looked up at Blue Stick. "Brock! I'm riding hard, Blue Stick. You best stay here."

With a single shake of his head, the old Comanche muttered. "I ride."

They rode, and they rode hard. Sweat poured down Cam's face, the heat of which irritated the poison ivy blisters on the side of his face. More than once in the next hour, they lost the trail, but for whatever reason, luck seemed to be running their way, for within minutes each time, they were back on the trail.

The sign was thin, a scar on a rock, a snapped limb, an overturned rock exposing its damp belly. Once or twice, Cam glimpsed a fleeting glance of his quarry in the distance.

Blue Stick fell behind, but stubbornly continued after Cam. Finally, they lost the trail altogether. Blue Stick rode up as Cam searched the rocky ground for any sign, at the same time scratching his swollen face. There was none. It was as if the ground had opened up and swallowed Joe Brock.

Joe Brock sneered as he lay on his belly on the rim, looking down on Cam and Blue Stick. He still puzzled over just what had taken place back in Menard for the sheriff to turn Cam loose, but after today, it wouldn't make any difference.

He cranked a cartridge in his Winchester, laid the front sight on Cam's chest, and slowly tightened his finger on the trigger.

Below, the old Indian suddenly drove his horse into Cam's at the same time Brock pulled the trigger. Cam's horse squealed and reared into the air, hooves frantically pawing. Cam leaped from the saddle as the horse toppled backward.

When he hit the ground, he rolled behind a rock. He looked around. Blue Stick's horse was down, its head tossed back, and its tongue dangling from between the animal's teeth. Beyond the dead horse, Blue Stick crouched behind a boulder.

Six-gun in hand, Cam pressed up against the granite upthrust behind which he had scrambled. He grimaced when he saw his horse hobbling about on three legs. The ugly twist in the animal's front leg told Cam it was broken.

Long minutes passed. To the east, the sky grew dark as the fingers of night reached out into the daylight. A distant sound rolled down the valley. He looked at Blue Stick who grunted, "He go."

Not taking a chance, they remained where they were until shadows filled the valley. To the north, clouds moved in, covering the stars.

Chapter Twenty-one

As night fell over the canyon, the rain began. Carrying what gear they could, Cam and Blue Stick found a small refuge under a layered ledge of white limestone where they built a fire for the night. Cam's stomach growled, so he took his belt up a notch, a practice he had fallen back on more than once when he was without grub.

During the night, the rain dropped the temperature several degrees, carrying with it a chill that drove straight to the bones. Blue Stick said nothing, just sat silently, staring at the fire with a blanket about his shoulders, seemingly oblivious to the cold.

Cam tried to sleep, but every time he drifted off, another gust of chilly air blasted him or a gust of rain whipped under the ledge.

The night was long and miserable. As the sky lightened, Cam's eyes popped open in surprise. He looked at Blue Stick, who had tilted his thin face so he could smell the air.

Pushing to his feet, Cam stepped out into the weather upwind from his own fire and drew a deep breath. There it was again. Wood smoke!

He ducked under the ledge. "Stay here."

Pulling his collar up around his neck, he headed upwind around the rocky bluff under which they had spent the night. The rain gave no indication of slacking.

The smell of wood smoke grew stronger. As he crept around the base of the ridge, he dropped into a crouch. Through the underbrush, a flash of dancing flames caught his eye. He crept forward until he stopped behind a small patch of cedar. He parted the branches.

His eyes grew wide. He scrubbed them with his fists, then looked again to be sure he wasn't hallucinating. His hopes soared. It was the Barrett wagon, and squatting around a fire beneath a fly were Milly and the children.

Then a frown creased his forehead. What were they doing out here? Why weren't they back in Limestone where she was supposed to be teaching?

He shook his head. He could find out later. Right now, he had to get Blue Stick into a shelter.

Twenty minutes later, Ira shouted and pointed into the rain. "Milly! Look! It's Cam and Blue Stick."

Stunned by the two men's sudden appearance out in the middle of the wilderness during the height of the storm, Milly was speechless.

Cam stopped outside the fly. "Sure would appreciate if we could come in. The old man is feeling mighty poorly."

Milly looked at Blue Stick, then back at Cam in disbelief. She pressed her hand to her lips when she saw the sling Cam wore. The sight galvanized her into action. "Bring him in. Hurry. Ira, put down a canvas over the mud."

Within minutes, Blue Stick was covered with blankets and Milly was holding a cup of hot stew to his lips.

Cam poured some coffee. "I'm mighty obliged, Miss Milly. After all that's happened."

She glanced over her shoulder and noticed the swollen cheek below his left temple. "Looks like more happened to you than us. Who shot you?"

"The soldier boys." Briefly, he related the events since he had escaped. "I ran Hez Clutter down in Cherry Springs. He said Brock was behind it all."

Keeping her eyes on Blue Stick, she replied. "I figured as much, but I wasn't sure. I never thought you or Patch were involved."

"Thanks."

"So, you figure Brock is the one who killed Clutter?"

"Reckon so. Makes sense. If Clutter reaches Menard, Brock's plan is blown up higher than a sun-fishing bronco."

"Now what?" Satisfied the old Comanche was resting easily, she turned to face Cam.

For the first time, he had a good look at her. He stiffened, surprised. Dark rings circled her eyes, and she appeared to have been crying. He answered her question. "I've got to get Brock. Make him confess."

"How are you going to do that?"

He frowned, truly puzzled by the weariness and pain etched across her face and the fact she had left Limestone. "I got me a plan of my own. But, what about you? What are you and the kids doing out here? You're supposed to be back in Limestone."

Ellie and Ira ducked their heads, but Milly looked Cam straight in the eye, her jaw set, her eyes unfeeling. The promise she had made to herself when the cowpokes back in Limestone were loading her wagon burned in her breast. In a firm, determined voice, she replied. "Because, Mister Cameron, my brother and sister and I are half-breeds. Our mother was Lipan. Our father was a white lawman in San Antonio." She glared at him, her eyes blazing with defiance.

The admission stunned Cam. Half-breed was the last thought that would occur in a body's mind when they looked at the Barretts. And it was indeed the last thing he would have surmised.

Embarrassed by his silence, Milly felt her cheeks burn, but she held her eyes fixed on his. "You're welcome to stay the night if you want."

He studied her a moment. "Well, Miss Milly, I reckon I see your problem. I got me a problem too, and the way I see it, hanging from a rope is a heap more of a problem than what you folks have. I reckon I know some of what folks think about you and those like you, but I'm not one of them. You've always been decent to everyone about you. You're a good person. I'd be plumb tickled if you'd permit me and Blue Stick the heat of your fire for the rest of the night."

For a moment, Milly remained transfixed. Then, tears filled her eyes. "You're telling me the truth? You don't mind being with us?"

Cam laughed. "Shucks, Miss Milly, my Pa never had nothing. We were the poor white trash living down in the barrios with the Mexicans in Tucson. No, ma'am. Like I said, I'm privileged that you let us stay." He paused, then added, "We had our horses shot from under us. I need to get to Menard where I can run Joe Brock down."

For a moment, Milly hesitated, casting a wary glance in the direction of Menard. Finally, she nodded, "I wasn't planning on heading in that direction, but under the circumstances, I'd be pleased to take you to Menard."

Slowly, the sky grew lighter, and the rain began to slack off. With Ira's help, Cam harnessed the team while Milly and Ellie packed and loaded their gear. By the time the wagon moved out with Blue Stick in the back, the rain had stopped.

The war party of Comanches struck an hour later.

Cam was unfamiliar with the narrow and twisting trace that wound southwest around, and sometimes over, the cedar and scrub oak-studded limestone hills and bluffs. He sat on the wagon bench beside Milly, who handled the team expertly.

He couldn't help noticing how her slender fingers held the reins ever so gently, sensing the horses's reactions instantly. Cam's brain burned with questions, but he held his tongue. He had seen the defiance in her eyes, and he knew from experience such defiance was the result of anger and pain.

He did not want to add to her pain. "What are your plans after Menard?"

Keeping her eyes on the narrow road ahead, she replied. "I planned to head up to Kickapoo Springs. See if I could find something up there for us."

Cam nodded, wishing he could somehow help her find a solution to her problems. He wanted to tell her he would help, but he had more trouble on his own tail than he could handle. He wouldn't be making any kind of plans for the next few years except how to dodge the law.

Suddenly, the wagon bed beneath his legs exploded, and then the roar of a rifle echoed across the rugged countryside. He looked up to see half-a-dozen mounted Comanches on the rim of the precipice beneath which the wagon was rolling.

Another shot rang out.

"Heeyaaa," Milly shouted, popping the reins on the horses's rumps. The animals leaped forward.

"Get down," Cam shouted, as the wagon careened along the narrow trail, unable to avoid the rocks in its path. He shucked his six-gun and fired at the screaming line of warriors recklessly descending the winding trail cut in the face of the sheer bluff. His chances of hitting one of the Comanches were as thin as rock soup.

The wagon rattled and bounced as they swept into a small clearing and then angled up the road, ascending a slope between two steep bluffs. At the top of the slope, the road abruptly dropped away. The wagon picked up speed. A rear wheel slammed into a boulder, and with a loud crack that sounded like a Sharps .54, the wheel shattered.

The axle slammed into the ground and the light wagon skidded to a halt.

"Out!" Cam shouted, looking around desperately for a place to fort up. He spotted a tumble of boulders beneath a ledge of white limestone. "Grab the guns. Make for that overhang."

As the others dashed for the boulders, Cam spun around and touched off three shots in the direction of the approaching Comanches. The cluster of horses split like a covey of quail, giving Cam time to follow the others behind the boulders.

Two Comanche warriors jumped into the wagon and began firing while the other four spread out behind large boulders and cedar.

Having removed his sling, Cam ordered, "Shoot the wagon." Grimacing against the pain, he pulled his Winchester into his shoulder and pumped four slugs into the wagon at the same time Milly and Blue Stick fired. After the barrage, one Comanche screamed, and the other leaped from the rear of the wagon, limping for the underbrush.

Blue Stick sent him sprawling to the ground.

"That's going to make them mighty mad," Cam muttered.

And they were, pouring lead at the bulwark of boulders in a frenzy. The slugs hummed overhead or slapped into the boulders harmlessly.

Cam and the others remained hunkered down, from time to time one or the other popping up to snap off one or two shots just to keep the Comanche at bay.

"You think they'll rush us?" Milly asked after snapping off a shot and ducking behind her boulder. Her face was flushed, but there was no fear in her green eyes.

Cam looked at Blue Stick. The old Comanche grunted. "When others come." He paused and looked around, studying the almost vertical cliff against which they had taken refuge.

"When will the others come?" Cam asked.

The old man shrugged. His words couched in fatalism. "When they come."

Milly and Cam exchanged wry grins.

The day wore on. Once Ellie complained of thirst. "Sorry," Cam said. "Canteens are in the wagon."

Occasionally, a heated exchange of gunfire broke out, but for the most part, the firing had been random, an ominous foreboding to Cam that the Comanche were simply biding their time until more warriors arrived.

Once, Cam spotted Milly with her eyes closed and her lips moving. "Include me in your prayer," he said with a crooked grin.

A light blush colored her cheeks. "I was praying for night." She glanced at his shoulder. "How is it?"

He touched it lightly. "Sore, but it hasn't started bleeding again."

Finally, the sun dropped below the crests of the rocky hills and the valley filled with shadows. As the last vestiges of daylight faded, Blue Stick crawled to Cam. "Moon come up late. We go."

Cam frowned. "Go? Where?"

The old man touched his chest, then gestured to a cluster of boulders closer to the cliff. "No noise. Plenty dark soon. Stay together." He removed a beaded belt and held to one end as he handed the other end to Milly indicating she was to follow him.

Cam looked at Milly, who arched an eyebrow. She shrugged. Cam nodded. "It might work. Go ahead and follow after him, Milly. Kids, stay with your sister, and no noise. Here." Cam cut his sling in three pieces and handed one to each child. "Hold tight. If it gets too dark, we can still follow each other."

For the next twenty minutes, the small party moved over the rocks through the darkness. From time to time, Cam glimpsed the tiny shadow that was Ira in front of him, but, for the most part, he simply followed wherever the taut strip of sling led. They were strung out like a centipede, its parts held together by pieces of cloth and strips of beads.

Ellie whined. "Milly, I'm scared."

"Shhh, Honey. You'll be fine. I'm right here, and your brother is right behind you."

The tiny girl sniffed, but remained silent.

Suddenly, Cam stumbled into Ira who had stopped. "What?" Cam whispered.

Blue Stick replied in a hushed voice. "We crawl here."

As they moved forward, Cam felt the air grow cool and the smell musty. Once or twice, walls brushed against his shoulders. Another time, when he raised his head, his hat struck rock. They were in a narrow tunnel. After a few minutes, Cam realized the tunnel was growing wider.

A few minutes later, Blue Stick whispered. "We stop. You stand."

Cam slowly rose, extending his arms, touching nothing but air. They were in some sort of chamber. Suddenly the spark of a flint punched a hole in the darkness. There was another spark, and another, and then a tiny flame came to life.

Within moments, a small fire illumined portions of the room in which they stood. Blue Stick deftly built two torches, touched them to the fire, and gave one to Cam. "Come."

He led the way through the darkness without hesitation. Beyond the weak glow of the flickering torches, complete darkness waited. Cam brought up the rear. He lost track of time, but suddenly, he heard the sound of running water.

Chapter Twenty-two

Blue Stick halted at the edge of a pool of water. "Drink," he said. "Good." While the others drank, he crossed the damp room and knelt. Within moments, a cheery fire blazed, illumining the cold, stark walls of the chamber.

The room was twelve to fifteen feet high and twice as wide. Hand-woven straw mats, long unused, lay about on the floor, providing a barrier against the damp and cold floor once the years of dust were shaken from them.

"What is this place?" Cam asked, peering around into the darkness beyond.

"Many times in the old days, Comanches hide from *los guardabosques*, the Rangers," Blue Stick grunted. "No more. Only I know of it."

"Well," Cam drawled, studying the darkness surrounding them. "At least we're safe and have water."

"I sure wish we had something to eat," Ira said in a whisper.

Cam ruffled the boy's hair. "Do what I do." He cinched up his belt a notch.

Ira frowned skeptically. "Will that help?"

"Well, it keeps your pants from falling down," he drawled, winking at Milly.

"Now, we sleep," Blue Stick announced.

Comfort is relative, but for the small party, lying on mats in front of a fire, snuggled down in their heavy coats, and out of the weather, they slept soundly.

When they awakened, Blue Stick sat motionless in front of the fire, broiling three rabbits on spits. Ravenous with hunger, the others made short work of the small animals. When Cam asked how Blue Stick came up with them, the old man explained. "I go out. Find rabbit. See Comanche. Many. They not go. We stay. Leave when dark."

The day passed slowly. Cam and Ira wandered about the chamber and into two adjoining rooms. In one of the rooms, Ira squatted and picked up a handful of odd-shaped rocks from a pile next to a wall. "I never seen rocks like this."

Cam rolled one over in his hand, inspecting it in the flickering light of the torch. About two inches long, it had the shape of some of those lava rocks back in Arizona. "Mighty heavy," he said, handing it back to Ira. He squatted and picked up a larger one, flat and about half the size of his hand. "I'm like you, boy. I never seen anything like this."

At that moment, Blue Stick called from the other room. "We go."

Without thinking, Cam dropped the flat rock in the pocket of his Mackinaw.

His bag strung over his shoulder, Blue Stick led them on a meandering course through the dark chambers for fifteen minutes. Suddenly, the flames of their torches leaped forward, drawn to an opening in the caverns.

Blue Stick halted, the darting flames of his torch illumining a recess a few feet deep in the wall. Above the recess was an opening. "We go up."

Cam could feel the air against the back of his neck as it was sucked up the chimney. Holding his torch under the opening to the chimney he peered upward. At least twenty feet. He looked at Ellie. "Blue Stick, you go first. Ira, you go next, then Milly."

Milly frowned. "What about Ellie?"

The lanky cowpoke grinned at the frightened girl. "She goes with me." He knelt. "Listen, honey. You're going to grab me around the neck and wrap your legs around my waist, and then the two of us are going to shinny right up to the top. Okay?"

She gulped, but nodded bravely.

Blue Stick disappeared up the chimney, and Ira followed. Bracing one foot against the chimney wall and his other foot against the opposite wall, Ira walked up just like a little monkey. Milly copied him. When she reached the top, she called down. "Come on up."

Cam dropped his torch on the chamber floor, then

eased into the chimney. He picked up Ellie and pulled her to his chest, wincing slightly as the healing wound in his shoulder throbbed. "Now, hang on. We're going up." His legs were too long for the leverage needed to ascend as the others. Instead, he leaned his back against one side of the chimney, bent his knees, and braced his feet on the far side. He took two small steps, paused, then, pressing his hands against the wall behind him, worked his shoulders upward. The ascent was painfully slow. Inch by inch, he moved one shoulder, then the other, followed by another step or two.

His progress was measured in inches, two-hundred-and-forty of them.

The rocks cut into his back and the palms of his hands. Sweat stung his eyes. His lungs burned. His legs began to cramp.

Just when he thought he might fall back down, hands lifted Ellie from his chest.

With a gasp of relief, he rolled out on the rock-strewn ground and sprawled on his back, sucking in great draughts of fresh air, flooding oxygen through his veins. Overhead, the stars glittered brightly. The most beautiful sight he had seen.

Blue Stick muttered. "Come."

Like nebulous wraiths, they ghosted through the darkness. From time to time, Cam glimpsed the stars through the canopy of leaves. Once, he caught sight of the Big Dipper to his right, which indicated Blue Stick was leading them west.

Finally, the old Comanche pulled up. In the bluish white glow of starlight, Cam saw the old man staring at a sheer bluff straight ahead.

"What is it?" Cam whispered.

"Bad storm come."

Milly gasped.

Blue Stick continued. "Come. We hide from storm. Come morning, we reach river. That direction." He pointed southwest.

Cam looked around the sharp hills of rugged rocks. "Hide? Where?"

Without replying, Blue Stick led them around a thick tangle of undergrowth and into another cave. "Wait." He knelt and quickly built a small fire with flint. Building a small torch, he studied the interior of the cave. With a satisfied grunt, he led the way inside. "Good. No *serpiente*."

Cam frowned. "No what?"

"Snakes," Milly said. "No snakes in here."

Cam arched an eyebrow.

Minutes later, a warm fire blazed.

The storm struck during the night, a blue norther howling in from the Artic. Luckily, the storm was a dry one, but the temperature had dropped to well below freezing.

The cave was small, and the heat of the fire reflected off the walls and roof, creating a snug space between the fire and the rear of the cave. The children were curled on their sides, sleeping deeply in their coats. Blue Stick was leaning against the wall, sleeping.

Absently, Cam reached inside his heavy coat, then grimaced when he remembered he was out of tobacco. He grinned shyly when he saw Milly watching him. "Habit," he muttered.

Milly smiled, then glanced away, suddenly feeling awkward, and not knowing why.

He looked at her, and for a moment, their eyes met and held. Embarrassed, they looked away at the same time.

"Sorry about the trouble we've caused," he blurted out, fiddling with a button on his coat.

"It was no trouble," Milly answered, staring at her hands folded in her lap. "I'm glad we could help."

He nodded. "So, you plan to teach up in Kickapoo Springs?"

She shrugged. "I don't know about teaching. Probably someone would come through and recognize us, and then we'd have to move on."

A wild, crazy idea struck him. "Have you ever thought about Arizona?"

"Arizona?" She looked up at him with a frown.

"Yes, ma'am. Arizona Territory. Wide open spaces and no one to tell a body what he can or can't do. No one going around looking down their noses at others."

She stared at him dreamy-eyed, a faint smile playing over her lips. "That would be just wonderful, but does such a place really exist?"

"Sure does. Up in the north of Arizona. Tall pines, mountains—why, some of those mountains are so high, snow stays on them year-round. And in the fall, the meadows are green and the trees are yellow."

With a trace of hope in her voice, she asked. "Is that where you're going?"

"I'd like to. If I can get all my troubles settled here."

"Just tell the sheriff the truth. Patch told me what happened. I believe him."

"Thanks." Cam chuckled and stared into the dancing flames. "The sheriff's the law, and the law needs proof. That's why I have to bring Joe Brock in."

"And then you'll go? I mean, on to Arizona."

He looked around at her. She was a mighty pretty young thing, much too good for a saddle tramp like him. He probably wouldn't have a chance with someone like her, but if he did, she deserved the truth. "I got another problem to settle. Back south, in La Grange, I got in with a bad crowd." Quickly, he detailed the events of the bank robbery and his efforts to repay the sum.

"Maybe the sheriff doesn't know about that."

With a rueful grin, Cam replied. "He knows."

"Maybe they'll go easy on you," she whispered when he finished. She wanted to say more but dared not. The feelings boiling inside of her were new and strange.

Giving his head a brief shake, he replied, "It'd be nice."

A thoughtful silence fell over them.

She studied him a moment longer, surprised that she was hoping the tall man would go on to Arizona. *Maybe*—She cut off her thoughts, knowing they could never be.

During the early morning hours, they drifted asleep.

When Cam awakened, he fed the fire and looked

around. Milly and the children were still slept. He looked at Blue Stick. The old man appeared not to have moved since the night before. Something about the Comanche elder looked out of place. Cam crawled over to the old Indian and laid his hand on the old man's arm. It was cold and stiff.

He looked into Blue Stick's face.

The old Comanche was dead.

He awakened the others, gave them the news, and, slipping the old Indian's bag from Blue Stick's thin shoulder, went about burying the old Comanche under a cairn of limestone rocks.

Before moving out, Cam inspected the buckskin bag. It was half full of the same kind of rocks Ira had collected. For a moment, he started to dump them but decided against it. He strung the bag over his shoulder.

Minutes later, they pulled out, heading southwest. The day was bitterly cold, but luck smiled on them and held back on the snow and ice.

They hit the San Saba two miles east of Menard just before dark. By the time they reached the outskirts of town, darkness had fallen over the small community. The only light came from the stars, which seemed to glow even brighter in the intense cold.

"What do we do now?" Milly whispered.

"Save for a few cowpokes, most folks is sitting down to supper. Streets are probably empty. But I reckon we best swing around behind. I want to see Doc Kelton."

"The doctor? Why?"

Keeping his eyes on the dim lights punching

holes in the darkness, he replied grimly. "He's the only one besides the sheriff I can trust."

"The sheriff? Why don't you go to him then?"

Cam shook his head, still keeping his eyes forward. "He'd have to jail me. Doc will look after you and the kids while I track Brock down."

Milly hesitated, and when she spoke, she couldn't believe the words coming from her lips. "After you find him, will you come back?"

He didn't move for a moment, and then he slowly turned and looked down at her. "I'd like to." He left unsaid the next question.

She answered it for him. "Good."

Chapter Twenty-three

Doctor Kelton hurried the four of them into his back room and quickly lowered the window shades. He frowned at Cam. "What the Sam Hill you doing here? The whole country is looking for you."

"Look, Doc. I know who pulled off the payroll robbery. I need a horse and time to run him down. The only witness I had got himself shot dead. I—"

Without warning, the door burst open, and Sheriff Luke Potter stood in the opening, his six-gun leveled on Cam's belly. "Just don't make no sudden moves, Cam. You hear?"

Milly gasped, and Ellie grabbed Milly around the waist and buried her face in her sister's breast. Ira rushed to Cam's side.

"Easy, Sheriff," Cam said in cautious voice. "Easy. I won't try nothing."

Potter shook his head. "I figured you'd be long out of the country by now." He grimaced. "I hoped you would be, son."

The lanky cowpoke grinned. "Got me some unfinished business."

"Hez Clutter?"

"He's dead. Brock killed him."

Potter nodded to Milly. "Patch told me the story this young woman passed on to him about Clutter and one of the payroll robbers."

"Clutter admitted Brock was behind it. He also admitted that Brock told the robbers to use my name because of the bank robbery down in La Grange. I was bringing him in to you when Brock ambushed us."

Arching an eyebrow, the sheriff grunted. "A body could say that was a might convenient ambush for you."

"Reckon they would. That's why I need Brock." Cam read the skepticism in the sheriff's eyes. "But there's a wild card in the hand, Sheriff. The payroll."

"The payroll?" Potter's leathery face wrinkled in a frown. "What are you driving at?"

"You told me there was ten thousand in the saddlebags. The outlaws, according to Clutter, only found two thousand." He paused to let the implication sink in.

After a moment, Potter replied. "Two thousand?"

"That's what he said, which means there's more to this than meets the eye. Why would someone put two thousand in the bag and spread word that it held ten?"

The sheriff arched an eyebrow. "He might have been lying."

"Might have, but I don't think so. I'll ask you again. Why would someone put two thousand in the bag and spread word that it held ten?"

Pursing his lips, Potter nodded thoughtfully.

Cam continued. "Brock is the only one who knows for sure. No one else looked in the saddlebags."

"He could have kept the rest for himself."

"But he killed the two men he thought had taken the eight thousand. Why did he do that? That's why I have to get to Brock—to clear me."

Potter remembered the two dead jaspers he had run across east of town. "Two men?"

"Yep. Went by the handles of Sundown and Blackjack."

Milly broke in. "The one I saw talking to Hez Clutter wore black clothes."

Nodding slowly, Potter recollected that one set of sliced-up duds that he had draped over one of the dead men had been black.

With a wry grin, Cam added. "Then I got me that problem down in La Grange."

Potter studied him a moment. The missing eight thousand answered the question he had been asking himself over and over. Until now, every theory he had pieced together fell apart, but now, he had the answer to the one question that had plagued him. What could Asplund or Higgins gain robbing from their own company? The answer? Eight thousand dollars and the outlaws who pulled the job took the blame for stealing the full amount.

With a wry grin, Sheriff Potter holstered his six-gun. "You take care of Brock; get him back here, and then I'll help you take care of La Grange."

Cam stared at Sheriff Potter in shock. Milly ran to Cam and threw her arms around his neck.

Potter added. "And I'll save you a heap of time

looking for that no-account critter. He passed through here headed to Kickapoo Springs."

Milly broke in. "Before you go, Cam, have the doctor look at your shoulder."

"Shoulder?"

Cam grinned sheepishly. "When I made my break from the soldiers."

"And Cam," said Sheriff Potter. "Don't say anything about the ten thousand to Brock, you hear?"

The lanky deputy frowned. "Why not?"

He gave Cam a sly grin. "I got me a plan."

During the ride to Kickapoo Springs, another cold front blew in, this one bringing first ice to coat the ground and then snow to make traveling even more dangerous. Cam rode with his head ducked into the wind and his heavy Mackinaw pulled up about his neck.

Kickapoo Springs was a small village along the creek of the same name. Its half-a-dozen or so buildings were fashioned of rocks and other materials that could be found locally with the exception of the saloon, which was built of rough-sawn wood hauled in from Waco.

Cam pulled up at the general store and, leaving the bag looped over the saddle horn, went inside, anxious to warm his hands and put himself around some grub.

"Mighty cold today," drawled the storeowner as Cam stood with his backside to the pot-bellied wood stove and speared a peach from the can he had just purchased. Overhead, the stovepipes running the length of the building glowed bright red, radiating heat along a narrow corridor of the room.

"Seen colder," he replied around a mouthful of peach. "But this'll do for me."

For the next few minutes, they jawed while Cam went through a second can of peaches.

"Looking for work?"

"Nope." Cam glanced at the dried-up little storeowner. "Looking for a man. Big man." He spread his arms, a knife in one hand, a can of peaches in the other. "Shoulders like this."

The little man shook his head. "Most drifters head for the saloon first. I ain't seen nobody like that. Could be Finas over at the saloon seen him."

Cam turned up the can and drank the juice. "Thanks."

Outside, Cam paused under the porch of the general store and stared across the narrow street at the saloon. The snow fell steadily. In just the few minutes he'd been inside, his horse, standing hipshot at the hitch rail, had snow sticking to him despite his body heat.

Halting outside the saloon, Cam attempted to peer through the windows, but they were fogged over. Taking a deep breath, he unbuttoned his coat and slid his six-gun up and down in its holster a few times. Cam had never seen Joe Brock pull leather. If push came to shove, he hoped he was fast enough for the owlhoot.

Only a handful of jaspers were in the saloon, half at the bar, half at tables playing poker. At the first sweep of the room, Cam didn't spot Brock. A second, more thorough study of the room also failed to find the big man. He breathed easier and approached the bar, figuring on a drink before he started asking questions. "Whiskey," he ordered, fishing a wadded greenback from his pocket and tossing it on the bar. "Leave the bottle. I need to warm up." He grinned at the rotund bartender.

The first drink burned on the way down. When it hit his belly, it lit a small fire that grew hotter with each succeeding drink. After three, he relaxed, and nursed the fourth. Just as he started to question the bartender, he heard a woman's laugh from behind.

Cam glanced at the mirror behind the bar and spotted Joe Brock with his arm around the laughing woman. They were descending the stairs. Quickly, he turned his face forward and dropped his hand to the butt of his six-gun.

Their footsteps drew closer. As soon as Brock passed, Cam would get the drop on him. He listened hard. The clomp of boots and the click of heels were coming up on his left. Another few seconds and—

The cold steel of a gun muzzle jammed into the back of his head. A cruel voice spoke. "Surprised to see you here, Deputy. You—"

Cam spun on his heel, at the same time throwing up his left arm to knock away the gun hand. A piercing flash of pain ripped through his shoulder as he stretched the new flesh covering his wound.

Grimacing against the excruciating pain in his arm, he slung his whiskey in Brock's face. He barely heard the roar of the six-gun or the shattering of the mirror behind the bar.

With both hands, he grabbed Brock's wrist and slammed his hand against the bar, jarring the six-gun from the outlaw's grasp.

With a left hand like a club, Brock beat at the back of Cam's head. Cam dropped into a crouch and lunged forward, digging his shoulder into Brock's midsection, driving the larger man away from the bar, and sending him crashing into an empty poker table.

The table splintered. They both sprawled to the floor.

Cam leaped to his feet and grabbed for his own six-gun. Just as he brought it up, Brock's gnarled fist filled his vision. Stars exploded in his head. He stumbled backward and threw his arms out in a desperate effort to maintain his balance. When he did, his six-gun flew from his hand.

He shook his head, trying to clear it. He heard a roar that sounded like an enraged bull. He blinked his eyes, trying to refocus them. As they cleared, he saw Brock, head down, shoulders hunched, great arms widespread, charging him like a crazed grizzly. "I'll break you in half," Brock growled between clenched teeth.

At the last second Cam jumped aside and, gripping his fists together, slammed Brock in the back, sending the larger man hurtling headfirst into the bar.

He bounced off the bar like a rubber ball, hit the floor on his backside, and rolled over and onto his feet in one smooth move that froze Cam for a moment, a moment too long for as the bearded outlaw came to his feet, he swung a roundhouse right.

Cam's head whipped aside. His body followed.

He sprawled across the bar on his belly, his ears ringing and lights flashing in his head. With the instinct of a cornered mountain lion, he leaped aside.

At that moment, Brock shattered a chair against the bar where Cam had been sprawled. The stunned cowpoke spun and swung a right cross. He felt his knuckles slam into a rock-hard jaw that for a second seemed like a slab of immovable granite but then gave way.

He shook his head. His vision cleared to see Brock skidding on his belly across the floor. Without hesitation, Cam leaped in the middle of the larger man's back with his knees and grabbed him under the chin and pulled his head back as far as he could, bending the outlaw's spine into a backward curve.

Grunting and straining, Brock tried to force his head forward. For several moments, it was a test of sheer strength between the two. The tendons in Brock's neck stood out, taut as guitar strings.

But Cam had the leverage. Between clenched teeth, he muttered. "Give it up, Brock. Or I'll snap your spine like a dry branch."

Groaning between his clenched teeth, the big man's body strained forward, his muscles quivering as they fought against the unrelenting pressure Cam was putting on him.

Gritting his teeth, Cam pulled harder.

Beneath him, Brock grunted. Futilely, he tried slamming his fists against Cam's legs, but there was no strength in the awkward blows.

"I can hold a heap longer than you, Brock. Give it up."

Finally, the big man relaxed. His body went limp, unresisting. Cam held his grip. He glanced up at the handful of hurty-gurty gals and cowpokes looking on. "All right, Brock," he growled. "Tell them who pulled off the payroll robbery."

His words came in gasps. "Don't—know—what you're—talking about."

Cam jerked the big man's head farther back. "Talk, or I'll snap your back in two, blast you. Talk!"

Brock groaned in pain. "All right, all right. I did. I did. Take it easy, Deputy. I planned the robbery."

Holding the tension on Brock, Cam looked up at the surrounding faces. "You all heard."

Several nodded.

He looked at the bartender. "Write down what you heard, and all of you sign it."

The rotund bartender nodded hurriedly and fished a piece of paper from beneath the bar and began scribbling.

Cam held Brock's chin a moment longer. He glanced around and spotted remnants of the shattered chair nearby. Abruptly, he released his grip and instantly jumped backward, squatting to grab the leg of the broken chair.

Like a striking snake, Brock rolled over and kicked out with his feet, hoping to catch the smaller man off-guard. Missing Cam, he rolled into a sitting position just in time for Cam to slam the outlaw between the eyes with the chair leg.

The big man fell back like a pole-axed steer.

Chapter Twenty-four

With Joe Brock's wrists bound to the saddle horn and his feet tied under the belly of his horse, the ride back to Menard was uneventful. They arrived well after dark.

Sheriff Potter eyed the bruises on Brock's face and those on Cam's. He grinned wryly. "Gave you some trouble, huh?"

"Some."

Potter locked Brock in the cell in which Patch had resided. "He's over at the hotel," the sheriff explained. He hooked his thumb at Brock. "You talk to Brock about the payroll?"

"He confessed over in Kickapoo Springs. Here are depositions from several witnesses who heard him." Cam handed Potter the depositions.

Potter read them, then glanced from under his eyebrows at Brock. "Purty much sews thing up tight for you, Mister Brock."

The big man sneered.

"Yep," the sheriff added, folding the depositions into his vest pocket. "Reckon the judge will go mighty hard on any jasper that steals ten thousand dollars in payroll."

Brock's eyes grew wide. "Ten thousand? What the blazes are you talking about?"

Innocently, Sheriff Potter turned to the surprised outlaw. "Why, the amount of payroll you stole. Ten thousand dollars worth."

The big man sputtered. His mouth worked, but no words came out. Finally, he managed to blurt out. "There wasn't no ten thousand dollars in them saddlebags, Sheriff. I'll swear to that."

"That's what I was told by the mine superintendent. Ten thousand."

Brock shook his head adamantly. "No, sir. No, sir. There was no ten thousand. There was two thousand. We heard talk there was ten in it, but when I opened them saddlebags, there was only two."

Potter pursed his lips. "Umm. Interesting. Very interesting."

Later, in Cam's hotel room, Potter studied him and Patch as they sat around a table. "I've got no proof, but I'm convinced that Asplund and Higgins planned the robbery. They figured out a slick way to pocket money intended for the mine and put the blame on someone else."

"You think the judge would give Brock a break if he testified against them?"

Potter shook his head. "No jury will take Brock's word against Asplund's or Higgins's."

"What we need is someway to make one of them confess." Cam observed.

Patch scratched the beard on his slender face. "My Pa always snookered me and my brothers by telling us that one said something he really didn't."

Cam and Potter frowned at Patch. "I don't follow," Potter said.

"I do," said Cam. "My old man did the same thing. Once my brother left the gate open to the corn patch. The cows got in. Pa was mad enough to bite a rattlesnake in two. Now, I hadn't figured on tattling on my brother, but when Pa told me that my brother said I did it—Well, sir, that got me boiling mad, and I told him the truth."

Potter nodded his understanding. "You know, that just might work. Higgins was in the Barrett wagon when Asplund told me there was ten thousand dollars in the payroll. What do you figure would happen if Higgins suddenly discovered that instead of ten thousand, there was twenty in the payroll?"

Cam's eyes lit. "Why, he'd figure that Asplund pocketed another ten thousand."

"Yeah," Patch chimed in. "He'd figure Asplund had snookered him."

"It just might work," the sheriff muttered.

Cam and Patch looked at the sheriff expectantly. Potter nodded slowly. "Now, here's what we'll do."

The next morning, Cam peered from the window of the sheriff's office as Sheriff Potter and Doctor Kelton made their way to the rear of the Limestone

Mining Company office across the snow-covered street.

He buttoned his heavy coat with the deputy's badge pinned on the chest and stepped out into the cold. He slogged through the slush to the mining office and, stomping the mud from his boots, went inside.

Behind the counter, mine foreman George Higgins looked up. His eyes went wide with surprise when he recognized Cam. He grabbed for his six-gun, but Cam held up his hand, then laid his fingers on the shiny star on his chest. "Take it easy, Mister Higgins. I'm not the one who stole your payroll. The sheriff has him in jail. He sent me to tell you that we brought the outlaw in last night, and we have a full confession."

Higgins' eyes narrowed. His mind raced, but he remained cool. "How do I know you're telling the truth?"

With a soft chuckle, Cam replied. "You think I'd be here if I stole the twenty thousand dollars Mister Asplund told the sheriff was in the saddlebags?"

"Twen—" Higgins' eyes bulged, but he managed to keep the surprise out of his voice. "Oh, yeah, yeah. I see your point." He forced a laugh.

"That's why the sheriff sent me over. To tell you we caught the thief, but we only recovered a little over a thousand dollars." He paused, then added. "Sorry about the rest. The sheriff said he figures the outlaws already gambled it away."

Higgins nodded. "Who did it?"

"Owlhoot by the name of Joe Brock. He's over in the jail right now. You want to see him?"

The mine foreman hesitated. He glanced at the door to Coby Asplund's office. "Later," he replied. "I'll come over later."

Cam touched his fingers to the brim of his John B. "I'll tell the sheriff. Take care."

"Yeah," Higgins grunted. "You too."

No sooner had the door closed behind Cam than George Higgins grabbed a six-gun from his desk drawer and charged into the mine superintendent's office. He slammed open the door and glared at the fat man behind the desk. "You chiseling little no-good."

Coby Asplund looked up in surprise.

Outside the rear window, Sheriff Potter and Doctor Kelton peered through the crack between the windowsill and the drawn shade as Higgins launched into his tirade.

"You dirty thief. I got me a good mind to blow your head off."

Stunned by Higgins' unexpected display of anger, Coby's eyes grew wide. "What the Sam Hill—"

"Don't go playing no games with me. I just found out about the payroll."

"What do you mean? You already knew about it. We've already made our split."

Outside, Potter and Kelton exchanged smug looks.

"That's what you say," Higgins retorted. "Our split. Ha. I get four thousand and you get fourteen."

Coby jumped up from his chair. "What do you mean fourteen?"

"I just found out the payroll was twenty thousand, not ten like you told me."

"You what?" He hesitated, then in a guttural voice, said. "You fool. Someon—"

The rear door burst open, and Sheriff Potter, all six feet of him, stood in the doorway, six-gun in hand. "Hold it there, boys. We've heard enough."

Higgins snapped off a wild shot, then leaped back through the open door into the front office. He raced to the front door and threw it open. He skidded to a halt. Directly in front of him stood Cam, his own Colt drawn.

"Hold it right there, Higgins," Cam said in a chilling voice. "Drop the hogleg."

His eyes wild, Higgins glanced over his shoulder, then looked back around at Cam. "You ain't taking me, Deputy," he growled between clenched teeth. He thumbed back the hammer and fired.

Cam threw himself aside when Higgins cocked his revolver. While in midair, he snapped off a shot. His slug caught Higgins in the side, sending the big man spinning to the boardwalk.

Before Cam could regain his feet, a six-gun boomed behind him. The snow at his side exploded.

"What the—"

He pushed to his feet and spun just as Joe Brock halted beside the water trough and swung the muzzle of his six-gun on Cam's belly. Cam jerked his Colt up, squeezing the trigger at the same time.

Both guns fired.

A powerful blow struck Cam in his lower abdomen. His leg buckled, and he fell backwards in the snow. Desperately, he thumbed back the hammer and aimed the Colt, but Brock had disappeared.

Cam struggled to sit up, and then he saw Brock's boots sticking out from behind the water trough. He clenched his teeth against the throbbing in his right side and sagged back into the snow.

"Cam!" Milly, followed by Ira and Ellie, ran through the snow to him. She dropped to her knees at his side, tears rolling down her cheeks. "Is it bad?" She grabbed Cam's hand and squeezed.

By now, Doctor Kelton was at Cam's side, quickly unbuttoning the coat and vest.

Cam blinked once or twice. "What about it, Doc? How bad is it?"

Doc Kelton sat back on his heels and scratched his head. After a moment, he grinned and leaned forward, slipping his hand in Cam's coat pocket. He pulled out the flat rock Cam had dropped in his coat pocket back in the caves and held it up. "Well, Deputy, you're going to have quite a bruise, but this—" He paused, studying the flat rock. "Whatever it is, it saved your life."

"You mean—" Milly began.

The doctor nodded. "He's fine. Have a good bruise. Be a little sore, but he's fine. The bullet hit this." He turned the hand-sized slab over in his hands. In the middle was an indention. He stuck his hand back in Cam's coat pocket and pulled out the spent slug.

Ira spoke up. "That's the rock Cam found in the cave."

Doc Kelton arched an eyebrow. "Doesn't look like a rock to me. See what I mean?" He handed the slab to Cam. When the slug hit the slab, it tore loose the corrosion coloring the slab. Beneath, it glittered of silver. "If I'm not mistaken, that's silver. Pure silver."

Chapter Twenty-five

Outside, the snow fell steadily. In the kitchen of Sheriff Potter's small house, the mouth-watering aroma of home-baked bread filled the room. "Reckon it will be a fine Christmas after all," he said.

Cam grinned at Milly, who was pulling the pan of bread from the oven. "I couldn't ask for anymore, Sheriff."

Milly sat the bread on the cabinet and glanced around at Sheriff Potter. "What do you really think they will do about the bank robbery, Sheriff? Will Cam have to go to jail?" She draped a dishtowel over the hot loaf.

Potter cut his eyes at Cam, then, teasing, asked. "Would you want him to?"

Her face turned red. She stammered for words.

Cam intervened. "You're embarrassing her, Sheriff."

Potter laughed. "I'm sorry. Just having some fun. But, seriously, there ain't much chance he'll go to jail, Miss Milly. I'll vouch for him. According to the sheriff down in La Grange, the outlaws got almost two thousand dollars. Cam here has sent about five hundred back, about a hundred more than his share. They got the rest of the money back when they caught the others."

"So the bank came out ahead," Cam observed.

The sheriff pulled out a bag of Bull Durham. "I wouldn't ask for it back if I was you," he replied. He winked at Milly. "What with the two thousand reward Coby Asplund offered, Cam, you'll have enough to make a nice down payment on a small ranch hereabouts. With the deputy's job and a small ranch, all you'll need is a family."

Milly's cheeks colored. Cam glanced at the floor, then sidelong at her. She smiled broadly, and the blush on her cheeks deepened.

"Don't forget the silver," Ira reminded them, pointing to the small stack of gray rocks in the middle of the table.

Sheriff Potter laughed. "That's right, son. Let's don't forget about the silver."

Later, sitting in front of the fireplace while their supper settled, Sheriff Potter cleared his throat. "You say there was a pile of those silver rocks in that cave, huh?"

"Yep." Cam kept his eyes on the flames leaping up the chimney. "One room almost full."

"Bowie's silver, I reckon," he drawled. "Heap of folks searched for it, but you're the only one I know who found it. Shame you don't remember where it was."

Cam glanced at Milly who smiled shyly. "Blue Stick led us every which way in the dark. All I can say it that it is three or four days back—northeast—I think," he added.

Ira looked up at Cam. "If you buy a ranch, Cam, can I be a cowboy for you?"

Embarrassed, Milly tried to hush her brother.

Cam chuckled, then looked at Milly. Their eyes met. He felt his cheeks burn, and he glanced at the floor. "Sure, boy." He lifted his gaze to Milly's soft brown eyes. "I reckon I'd like for it to be our ranch, stock it with a good breed of cows."

The smile on Milly's face blossomed.

That was answer enough for Cam.

Ira spoke up. "But, won't that cost a lot of money?"

Cam cut his eyes to the bag hanging on a peg on the far wall. He grinned to himself at the contents, at least three double handfuls of gray rocks. He shifted his gaze back to Milly, and he spoke to Ira. "Go get Blue Stick's bag yonder on the wall."

"Sure." Ira scampered across the room. "What for?" He pulled it off the peg, and it slammed to the floor. "Whew. This sure is heavy."

"Give it to your big sister. I don't reckon it's too soon for her first wedding gift."

Ira plopped the bag down in her lap. When she opened it, the frown on her face turned into disbelief. She spilled the contents on the table, a pile of gray rocks. Milly looked at Cam in stunned disbelief.

Cam nodded. "And maybe we'll buy some horses too."